Eight Tales of Terror

by EDGAR ALLAN POE

SCHOLASTIC INC.
New York Toronto London Auckland Sydney

ISBN 0-590-41136-5

12 11 10 9 8 7   9/8 0 1/9

Printed in the U.S.A   01

CONTENTS

A WORD TO THE READER

If Edgar Allan Poe had been asked to fill out an application blank, say at the age of twenty-one, it might have looked like this:

DATE OF BIRTH	January 19, 1809
PLACE OF BIRTH	Boston, Massachusetts
EDUCATION	Grammar School: Irvine, Scotland (1815) Sloane Street, London (1815-16) Manor House School, Stoke Newington, England (1817-20) Preparatory School:

	Richmond, Virginia (1820-25)
	College: University of Virginia (1826, February to December)
MILITARY SERVICE	U. S. Army, Fort Moultrie, South Carolina, and Fortress Monroe, Virginia (May 26, 1827 — April 15, 1829), sergeant major, honorable discharge
PARENTS	Deceased
GUARDIAN	Mr. John Allan, Richmond, Virginia
MARITAL STATUS	Single
PUBLICATIONS	*Tamerlane and Other Poems* (1827) *Al Aaraaf, Tamberlane, and Minor Poems* (1829)

Anyone examining such an application would be curious as to why he stayed so short a time at the University of Virginia. He might ask questions about the guardianship of Mr. John Allan; he would wonder, perhaps, why there had been no legal adoption. And he would be puzzled by the army career and the poetry: poets are not associated with military careers, as a rule. In short, he would make very little sense of the information as given.

If the "Poe" file were allowed to lapse for another twenty-one years, there would be no point in bringing it up to date. Mr. Poe would have been dead two years.

What had he done since his twenty-first birthday? At twenty-one he had been appointed to the United States Military Academy at West Point; at twenty-two he had been dismissed for disobedience and neglect of his duties as a cadet. He was still twenty-two when Mr. John Allan, his guardian, refused to have anything more to do with him. At twenty-six he had begun working for magazines. He had been a magazine editor (four different magazines) over a total period of six years. He had supported an ailing wife for twelve years. And he had written enough to fill seventeen volumes (his collected works). For a man who never had any money or leisure, a man who has been called an alcoholic, a dope addict, and a would-be suicide, his volume of work is amazing! The truth is that the legend of Edgar Allan Poe does not fit the facts, that his personal life was actually rather dull, and that he has himself to thank for parts of the image that has grown up around his name. He was fond of acting out roles that lent him an air of mystery. But his problems were real, and his attempts to solve them were largely unsuccessful.

Why did he write what he wrote? Part of the answer to this question is that he wrote for money. If he had not earned a little money, he would have starved to death — as he almost did. At the very end of his career, less than a week before his death, he wrote: "I have been invited out a great deal — but could seldom go, on account of not having a dress coat." It has to be said that he might have been better off financially if he had not written so candidly about certain writers and editors of his time. Here is a sample:

Mr. Briggs has never composed in his
life three consecutive sentences of gram-
matical English. He is grossly unedu-
cated.

To say that he wrote for money is not to
explain Edgar Allan Poe. There is more,
much more. But it is time that he was given
credit for being a professional writer, a man
who lived by his pen.

He wrote for the magazine readers of his
day, and his stories are not unlike the stories
of other contributors. At twenty-five he was
expressing his low opinion of what other
writers wrote; meanwhile, he was writing
nonsensical imitations of cheap magazine fic-
tion. By the time he was thirty, he had convinced himself that the brief narrative was
not something to make fun of; he had written
"Ligeia" and "The Fall of the House of
Usher," two serious works of art. By then he
saw a splendid future for the short story.

As a writer of magazine stories, Poe was
very conscious of his audience, and he wanted
to get certain responses from his readers.
Unlike Alfred Hitchcock, he could not make
a mystery or horror film. He had to depend

on words. Sometimes, for the modern reader, the words get in the way; the sentences are long, and the vocabulary is difficult. But the fact that he is read as much as he is, especially by young people, proves that he did not misjudge his audience, that he still can produce "a certain unique or single effect" in the minds of his readers. His language is nineteenth century, but his "unreal" world is the location of every horror picture, of every mystery program on television.

Just as movies of the weird and the fantastic take us out of the real world, so Poe's language keeps us from seeing his characters and situations as related to real life. The characters are like figures moving across a carefully prepared stage; often they are less important than the painted backdrop — a Fiberglas curtain that makes everything soft and dreamlike. This is as it should be. If the audience (the reader) gets close enough to suspect that Ligeia or Madeline Usher might have to get breakfast or sew on a button or meet somebody at the station, Poe's spell is broken and the tale becomes farce comedy. For Poe, distance is preserved by language. The style and tone that appear heavy and ornate are part of his intent: never to let us down to street level, never to suggest that the strange world of his stories is in any way related to the clutter of our daily lives.

JOHN P. ROBERTS
Montclair (N. J.) State College

The Cask of Amontillado

First published in *Godey's Lady's Book* for November, 1846, "The Cask" is perhaps the most widely read of all the Poe tales. Why? Can its popularity be traced to our own childish urge to "get even," to make someone pay for ignoring us? Montresor hates Fortunato — that much is certain; but we are never told the details of the "thousand injuries."

We are much impressed with Montresor's diabolical strategy as he lures his victim into the deepest recesses of the catacombs . . . as he executes the perfect crime. Our sadistic impulses are given full sway, even though we identify somewhat with Fortunato in his extreme anguish. We have a picture in our minds of what it means to be walled up and left to die. We may even allow him a drop of sympathy, if we are not completely captivated by Montresor's *"Nemo me impune lacessit"* (No one attacks me with impunity).

1

The thousand injuries of Fortunato I had borne as I best could; but when he ventured upon insult, I vowed revenge. You, who so well know the nature of my soul, will not suppose, however, that I gave utterance to a threat. *At length* I would be avenged; this was a point definitely settled — but the very definitiveness with which it was resolved precluded the idea of risk. I must not only punish, but punish with impunity. A wrong is unredressed when retribution overtakes its redresser. It is equally unredressed when the avenger fails to make himself felt as such to him who has done the wrong.

It must be understood that neither by word nor deed had I given Fortunato cause to doubt my good will. I continued, as was my wont, to smile in his face, and he did not perceive that my smile *now* was at the thought of his immolation.

He had a weak point — this Fortunato — although in other regards he was a man to be respected and even feared. He prided himself on his connoisseurship in wine. Few Italians have the true virtuoso spirit. For the most part their enthusiasm is adopted to suit the time and opportunity — to practice imposture upon the British and Austrian *millionaires*. In painting and gemmary, Fortunato, like his countrymen, was a quack — but in the matter of old wines he was sincere. In this respect I did not differ from him materially: I was skillful in the Italian vintages myself, and bought largely whenever I could.

It was about dusk, one evening during the supreme madness of the carnival season, that I encountered my friend. He accosted me with excessive warmth, for he had been drinking much. The man wore motley. He had on a tight-fitting parti-striped dress, and his head was surmounted by the conical cap and bells. I was so pleased to see him that I thought I should never have done wringing his hand.

I said to him: "My dear Fortunato, you are luckily met. How remarkably well you are looking today! But I have received a pipe of what passes for Amontillado, and I have my doubts."

"How?" said he. "Amontillado? A pipe? Impossible! And in the middle of the carnival!"

"I have my doubts," I replied; "and I was silly enough to pay the full Amontillado price without consulting you in the matter. You were not to be found, and I was fearful of losing a bargain."

"Amontillado!"

"I have my doubts."

"Amontillado!"

"And I must satisfy them."

"Amontillado!"

"As you are engaged, I am on my way to Luchesi. If anyone has a critical turn, it is he. He will tell me — "

"Luchesi cannot tell Amontillado from Sherry."

"And yet some fools will have it that his taste is a match for your own."

"Come, let us go."

"Whither?"

"To your vaults."

"My friend, no; I will not impose upon your good nature. I perceive you have an engagement. Luchesi — "

"I have no engagement; — come."

"My friend, no. It is not the engagement, but the severe cold with which I perceive you are afflicted. The vaults are insufferably damp. They are encrusted with niter."

"Let us go, nevertheless. The cold is merely nothing. Amontillado! You have been imposed upon. And as for Luchesi, he cannot distinguish Sherry from Amontillado."

Thus speaking, Fortunato possessed himself of my arm. Putting on a mask of black silk, and drawing a *roquelaire* closely about my person, I suffered him to hurry me to my palazzo.

There were no attendants at home; they had absconded to make merry in honor of the time. I had told them that I should not return until the morning, and had given them explicit orders not to stir from the house. These orders were sufficient, I well knew, to insure their immediate disappearance, one and all, as soon as my back was turned.

I took from their sconces two flambeaux, and giving one to Fortunato, bowed him through several suites of rooms to the archway that led into the vaults. I passed down a long and winding staircase, requesting him to be cautious as he followed. We came at length to the foot of the descent, and stood together on the damp ground of the catacombs of the Montresors.

The gait of my friend was unsteady, and the bells upon his cap jingled as he strode.

"The pipe?" said he.

"It is farther on," said I; "but observe the white webwork which gleams from these cavern walls."

He turned toward me, and looked into my eyes with two filmy orbs that distilled the rheum of intoxication.

"Niter?" he asked, at length.

"Niter," I replied. "How long have you had that cough?"

"Ugh! ugh! ugh! — ugh! ugh! ugh! — ugh! ugh! ugh! — ugh! ugh! ugh! — ugh! ugh! ugh!"

My poor friend found it impossible to reply for many minutes.

"It is nothing," he said, at last.

"Come," I said, with decision, "we will go back; your health is precious. You are rich, respected, admired, beloved; you are happy, as once I was. You are a man to be missed. For me it is no matter. We will go back; you will be ill and I cannot be responsible. Besides, there is Luchesi — "

"Enough," he said; "the cough is a mere nothing; it will not kill me. I shall not die of a cough."

"True — true," I replied; "and, indeed, I had no intention of alarming you unnecessarily; but you should use all proper caution. A draught of this Medoc will defend us from the damps."

Here I knocked off the neck of a bottle which I drew from a long row of its fellows that lay upon the mould.

"Drink," I said, presenting him the wine.

He raised it to his lips with a leer. He paused and nodded to me familiarly, while his bells jingled.

"I drink," he said, "to the buried that repose around us."

"And I to your long life."

He again took my arm, and we proceeded.

"These vaults," he said, "are extensive."

"The Montresors," I replied, "were a great and numerous family."

"I forget your arms."

"A huge human foot d'or, in a field azure; the foot crushes a serpent rampant whose fangs are imbedded in the heel."

"And the motto?"

"Nemo me impune lacessit."

"Good!" he said.

The wine sparkled in his eyes and the bells jingled. My own fancy grew warm with the Medoc. We had passed through walls of piled bones, with casks and puncheons intermingling, into the inmost recesses of the catacombs. I paused again, and this time I made bold to seize Fortunato by an arm above the elbow.

"The niter!" I said; "see, it increases. It hangs like moss upon the vaults. We are below the river's bed. The drops of moisture trickle among the bones. Come, we will go back ere it is too late. Your cough — "

"It is nothing," he said; "let us go on. But first, another draught of the Medoc."

I broke and reached him a flagon of De Grâve. He emptied it at a breath. His eyes flashed with a fierce light. He laughed and threw the bottle upward with a gesticulation I did not understand.

I looked at him in surprise. He repeated the movement — a grotesque one.

"You do not comprehend?" he said.

"Not I," I replied.

"Then you are not of the brotherhood."

"How?"

"You are not of the masons."

"Yes, yes," I said; "yes, yes."

"You? Impossible! A mason?"

"A mason," I replied.

"A sign," he said.

"It is this," I answered, producing a trowel from beneath the folds of my *roquelaire*.

"You jest," he exclaimed; recoiling a few paces. "But let us proceed to the Amontillado."

"Be it so," I said, replacing the tool beneath the cloak, and again offering him my arm. He leaned upon it heavily. We continued our route in search of the Amontillado. We passed through a range of low arches, descended, passed on, and descending again, arrived at a deep crypt, in which the foulness of the air caused our flambeaux rather to glow than flame.

At the most remote end of the crypt there appeared another less spacious. Its walls had been lined with human remains, piled to the vault overhead, in the fashion of the great catacombs of Paris. Three sides of this interior crypt were still ornamented in this manner. From the fourth the bones had been thrown down, and lay promiscuously upon the earth, forming at one point a mound of some size. Within the wall thus exposed by the displacing of the bones, we perceived a still interior recess, in depth about four feet, in width three, in height six or seven. It seemed to have been constructed for no especial use within itself, but formed merely the interval between two of the colossal supports of the roof of the catacombs, and was backed by one of their circumscribing walls of solid granite.

It was in vain that Fortunato, uplifting his dull torch, endeavored to pry into the depth of the recess. Its termination the feeble light did not enable us to see.

"Proceed," I said; "herein is the Amontillado. As for Luchesi — "

"He is an ignoramus," interrupted my friend, as he stepped unsteadily forward, while I followed immediately at his heels. In an instant he had reached the extremity of the niche, and finding his progress arrested by the rock, stood stupidly bewildered. A moment more and I had fettered him to the granite. In its surface were two iron staples, distant from each other about two feet, horizontally. From one of these depended a short chain, from the other a padlock. Throwing the links about his waist, it was but the work of a few seconds to secure it. He was too much astounded to resist. Withdrawing the key, I stepped back from the recess.

"Pass your hand," I said, "over the wall; you cannot help feeling the niter. Indeed it is *very* damp. Once more let me *implore* you to return. No? Then I must positively leave you. But I must first render you all the little attentions in my power."

"The Amontillado!" ejaculated my friend, not yet recovered from his astonishment.

"True," I replied; "the Amontillado."

As I said these words I busied myself among the pile of bones of which I have before spoken. Throwing them aside, I soon uncovered a quantity of building stone and mortar. With these materials and with the aid of my trowel, I began vigorously to wall up the entrance of the niche.

I had scarcely laid the first tier of the masonry when I discovered that the intoxication of Fortunato had in a great measure worn off. The earliest indication I had of this was a low moaning cry from the depth of the recess. It was *not* the cry of a drunken man. There was then a long and obstinate silence. I laid the second tier, and the third, and the fourth; and then I heard the furious vibrations of the chain. The noise lasted for several minutes, during which, that I might hearken to it with the more satisfaction, I ceased my labors and sat down upon the bones. When at last the clanking subsided, I resumed the trowel, and finished without interruption the fifth, the sixth, and the seventh tier. The wall was now nearly upon a level with my breast. I again paused, and holding the flambeaux over the mason work, threw a few feeble rays upon the figure within.

A succession of loud and shrill screams, bursting suddenly from the throat of the chained form, seemed to thrust me violently back. For a brief moment I hesitated — I trembled. Unsheathing my rapier, I began to grope with it about the recess; but the thought of an instant reassured me. I placed my hand upon the solid fabric of the catacombs, and felt satisfied. I reapproached the wall. I replied to the yells of him who clamored. I re-echoed — I aided — I surpassed them in volume and in strength. I did this, and the clamorer grew still.

It was now midnight, and my task was drawing to a close. I had completed the eighth, the ninth, and the tenth tier. I had finished a portion of the last and the eleventh; there remained but a single stone to be fitted and plastered in. I struggled with its weight; I placed it partially in its destined position. But now there came from out the niche a low laugh that erected the hairs upon my head. It was succeeded by a sad voice, which I had difficulty in recognizing as that of the noble Fortunato. The voice said —

"Ha ha! ha! — he! he! — a very good joke indeed — an excellent jest. We will have many a rich laugh about it at the palazzo — he! he! he! — over our wine — he! he! he!"

"The Amontillado!" I said.

"He! he! he! — he! he! he! — yes, the Amontillado. But is it not getting late? Will not they be awaiting us at the palazzo, the Lady Fortunato and the rest? Let us be gone."

"Yes," I said, "let us be gone."

"For the love of God, Montresor!"

"Yes," I said, "for the love of God!"

But to these words I hearkened in vain for a reply. I grew impatient. I called aloud:

"Fortunato!"

No answer. I called again:

"Fortunato!"

No answer still. I thrust a torch through the remaining aperture and let it fall within. There came forth in return only a jingling of the bells. My heart grew sick — on account of the dampness of the catacombs. I hastened to make an end of my labor. I forced the last stone into its position; I plastered it up. Against the new masonry I re-erected the old rampart of bones. For the half of a century no mortal has disturbed them. *In pace requiescat!*

Hop-Frog

This story appeared in 1849 a few months before Poe's death, in the periodical *Flag of Our Union* for March 17. Like "The Cask of Amontillado," published three years earlier, "Hop-Frog" is about revenge, but here we know the cause; we are allowed to witness the insult to human dignity which prompts Hop-Frog's retaliation. There is no doubt where our sympathies lie — with the weak, defenseless little people who exact such a fearful price for their humiliation.

I never knew any one so keenly alive to a joke as the king was. He seemed to live only for joking. To tell a good story of the joke kind, and to tell it well, was the surest road to his favor. Thus it happened that his seven ministers were all noted for their accomplishments as jokers. They all took after the king, too, in being large, corpulent, oily men, as well as inimitable jokers. Whether people grow fat by joking, or whether there is something in fat itself which predisposes to a joke, I have never been quite able to determine; but certain it is that a lean joker is a *rara avis in terris*.

About the refinements, or, as he called them, the "ghosts" of wit, the king troubled himself very little. He had an especial admiration for *breadth* in a jest, and would often put up with *length*, for the sake of it. Overniceties wearied him. He would have preferred Rabelais' *Gargantua* to the *Zadig* of Voltaire: and, upon the whole, practical jokes suited his taste far better than verbal ones.

At the date of my narrative, professing jesters had not altogether gone out of fashion at court. Several of the great continental "powers" still retained their "fools," who wore motley, with caps and bells, and who were expected to be always ready with sharp witticisms, at a moment's notice, in consideration of the crumbs that fell from the royal table.

Our king, as a matter of course, retained his "fool." The fact is, he *required* something in the way of folly — if only to counterbalance the heavy wisdom of the seven wise men who were his ministers — not to mention himself.

His fool, or professional jester, was not *only* a fool, however. His value was trebled in the eyes of the king by the fact of his being also a dwarf and a cripple. Dwarfs were as common at court, in those days, as fools; and

many monarchs would have found it difficult
to get through their days (days are rather
longer at court than elsewhere) without both
a jester to laugh *with* and a dwarf to laugh
at. But, as I have already observed, your
jesters, in ninety-nine cases out of a hundred,
are fat, round, and unwieldy — so that it was
no small source of self-gratulation with our
king that, in Hop-Frog (this was the fool's
name), he possessed a triplicate treasure in
one person.

I believe the name "Hop-Frog" was *not*
that given to the dwarf by his sponsors at
baptism, but it was conferred upon him by
general consent of the seven ministers, on
account of his inability to walk as other men
do. In fact, Hop-Frog could only get along
by a sort of interjectional gait — something
between a leap and a wriggle — a movement
that afforded illimitable amusement, and of
course consolation, to the king, for (notwithstanding the protuberance of his stomach
and a constitutional swelling of the head)
the king, by his whole court, was accounted
a capital figure.

But although Hop-Frog, through the dis-
tortion of his legs, could move only with

great pain and difficulty along a road or floor, the prodigious muscular power which nature seemed to have bestowed upon his arms, by way of compensation for deficiency in the lower limbs, enabled him to perform many feats of wonderful dexterity, where trees or ropes were in question, or anything else to climb. At such exercises he certainly much more resembled a squirrel, or small monkey, than a frog.

I am not able to say, with precision, from what country Hop-Frog originally came. It was from some barbarous region, however, that no person ever heard of — a vast distance from the court of our king. Hop-Frog, and a young girl very little less dwarfish than himself (although of exquisite proportions, and a marvelous dancer), had been forcibly carried off from their respective homes in adjoining provinces, and sent as presents to the king, by one of his ever-victorious generals.

Under these circumstances, it is not to be wondered at that a close intimacy arose between the two little captives. Indeed, they soon became sworn friends. Hop-Frog, who, although he made a great deal of sport, was

by no means popular, had it not in his power
to render Trippetta many services; but *she*,
on account of her grace and exquisite beauty
(although a dwarf), was universally admired
and petted; so she possessed much influence,
and never failed to use it, whenever she
could, for the benefit of Hop-Frog.

On some grand state occasion — I forget
what — the king determined to have a masquerade; and whenever a masquerade, or
anything of that kind, occurred at our court,
then the talents both of Hop-Frog and Trippetta were sure to be called into play. Hop-
Frog, in especial, was so inventive in the way
of getting up pageants, suggesting novel
characters, and arranging costume, for
masked balls, that nothing could be done, it
seems, without his assistance.

The night appointed for the *fête* had arrived. A gorgeous hall had been fitted up,
under Trippetta's eye, with every kind of
device which could possibly give *éclat* to a
masquerade. The whole court was in a fever
of expectation. As for costumes and characters, it might well be supposed that every-
body had come to a decision on such points.
Many had made up their minds (as to what

roles they should assume) a week, or even a
month, in advance; and, in fact, there was not
a particle of indecision anywhere — except
in the case of the king and his seven ministers. Why *they* hesitated I never could tell,
unless they did it by way of a joke. More
probably, they found it difficult, on account
of being so fat, to make up their minds. At
all events, time flew; and, as a last resort,
they sent for Trippetta and Hop-Frog.

When the two little friends obeyed the
summons of the king, they found him sitting
at his wine with the seven members of his
cabinet council; but the monarch appeared
to be in a very ill humor. He knew that Hop-
Frog was not fond of wine; for it excited
the poor cripple almost to madness, and madness is no comfortable feeling. But the king
loved his practical jokes, and took pleasure
in forcing Hop-Frog to drink and (as the
king called it) "to be merry."

"Come here, Hop-Frog," said he, as the
jester and his friend entered the room;
"swallow this bumper to the health of your
absent friends [here Hop-Frog sighed] and
then let us have the benefit of your invention.
We want characters — *characters*, man —

something novel — out of the way. We are wearied with this everlasting sameness. Come drink! the wine will brighten your wits."

Hop-Frog endeavored, as usual, to get a jest in reply to these advances from the king; but the effort was too much. It happened to be the poor dwarf's birthday, and the command to drink to his "absent friends" forced the tears to his eyes. Many large, bitter drops fell into the goblet as he took it, humbly, from the hand of the tyrant.

"Ah! ha! ha! ha!" roared the latter, as the dwarf reluctantly drained the beaker. "See what a glass of good wine can do! Why, your eyes are shining already!"

Poor fellow! his large eyes *gleamed,* rather than shone; for the effect of wine on his excitable brain was not more powerful than instantaneous. He placed the goblet nervously on the table, and looked round upon the company with a half-insane stare. They all seemed highly amused at the success of the king's *"joke."*

"And now to business," said the prime minister, a *very* fat man.

"Yes," said the king. "Come, Hop-Frog, lend us your assistance. Characters, my fine fellow; we stand in need of characters — all of us — ha! ha! ha!" and as this was seriously meant for a joke, his laugh was chorused by the seven.

Hop-Frog also laughed, although feebly and somewhat vacantly.

"Come, come," said the king, impatiently, "have you nothing to suggest?"

"I am endeavoring to think of something *novel*," replied the dwarf, abstractedly, for he was quite bewildered by the wine.

"Endeavoring!" cried the tyrant, fiercely; "what do you mean by *that*? Ah, I perceive. You are sulky, and want more wine. Here, drink this!" and he poured out another goblet full and offered it to the cripple, who merely gazed at it, gasping for breath.

"Drink, I say!" shouted the monster, "or by the fiends — "

The dwarf hesitated. The king grew purple with rage. The courtiers smirked. Trippetta, pale as a corpse, advanced to the monarch's seat, and falling on her knees before him, implored him to spare her friend.

The tyrant regarded her, for some moments, in evident wonder at her audacity. He seemed quite at a loss what to do or say —

how most becomingly to express his indignation. At last, without uttering a syllable, he pushed her violently from him and threw the contents of the brimming goblet in her face.

The poor girl got up as best she could and, not daring even to sigh, resumed her position at the foot of the table.

There was a dead silence for about half a minute, during which the falling of a leaf, or of a feather, might have been heard. It was interrupted by a low, but harsh and protracted *grating* sound which seemed to come at once from every corner of the room.

"What — what — *what* are you making that noise for?" demanded the king, turning furiously to the dwarf.

The latter seemed to have recovered, in great measure, from his intoxication, and looking fixedly but quietly into the tyrant's face, merely ejaculated:

"I — I? How could it have been me?"

"The sound appeared to come from without," observed one of the courtiers. "I fancy it was the parrot at the window, whetting his bill upon his cage wires."

"True," replied the monarch, as if much

relieved by the suggestion; "but, on the honor of a knight, I could have sworn that it was the gritting of this vagabond's teeth."

Hereupon the dwarf laughed (the king was too confirmed a joker to object to anyone's laughing), and displayed a set of large, powerful, and very repulsive teeth. Moreover, he avowed his perfect willingness to swallow as much wine as desired. The monarch was pacified; and having drained another bumper with no very perceptible ill effect, Hop-Frog entered at once, and with spirit, into the plans for the masquerade.

"I cannot tell what was the association of idea," observed he, very tranquilly, and as if he had never tasted wine in his life, "but *just after* your majesty had struck the girl and thrown the wine in her face — *just after* your majesty had done this, and while the parrot was making that odd noise outside the window, there came into my mind a capital diversion — one of my own country frolics — often enacted among us, at our masquerades: but here it will be new altogether. Unfortunately, however, it requires a company of eight persons, and — "

"Here we *are*!" cried the king, laughing

at his acute discovery of the coincidence;
"eight to a fraction — I and my seven ministers. Come! what is the diversion?"

"We call it," replied the cripple, "the Eight
Chained Orangutans, and it really is excellent
sport if well enacted."

"*We* will enact it," remarked the king,
drawing himself up, and lowering his eyelids.

"The beauty of the game," continued Hop-
Frog, "lies in the fright it occasions among
the women."

"Capital!" roared in chorus the monarch
and his ministry.

"I will equip you as orangutans," proceeded
the dwarf; "leave all that to me. The resemblance shall be so striking that the company
of masqueraders will take you for real beasts
— and, of course, they will be as much terrified as astonished."

"Oh, this is exquisite!" exclaimed the king.
"Hop-Frog! I will make a man of you."

"The chains are for the purpose of increasing the confusion by their jangling. You are
supposed to have escaped, *en masse,* from
your keepers. Your majesty cannot conceive
the *effect* produced, at a masquerade, by eight
chained orangutans, imagined to be real ones

by most of the company; and rushing in with savage cries, among the crowd of delicately and gorgeously habited men and women. The *contrast* is inimitable."

"It *must* be," said the king; and the council arose hurriedly (as it was growing late), to put in execution the scheme of Hop-Frog.

His mode of equipping the party as orangutans was very simple, but effective enough for his purposes. The animals in question had, at the epoch of my story, very rarely been seen in any part of the civilized world; and as the imitations made by the dwarf were sufficiently beastlike and more than sufficiently hideous, their truthfulness to nature was thus thought to be secured.

The king and his ministers were first encased in tight-fitting stockinet shirts and drawers. They were then saturated with tar. At this stage of the process, some one of the party suggested feathers; but the suggestion was at once overruled by the dwarf, who soon convinced the eight, by ocular demonstration, that the hair of such a brute as the orangutan was much more efficiently represented by *flax*. A thick coating of the latter was accordingly plastered upon the coating of tar.

A long chain was now procured. First, it was passed about the waist of the king, *and tied*; then about another of the party, and also tied; then about all successively, in the same manner. When this chaining arrangement was complete, and the party stood as far apart from each other as possible, they formed a circle; and to make all things appear natural, Hop-Frog passed the residue of the chain, in two diameters, at right angles, across the circle, after the fashion adopted, at the present day, by those who capture chimpanzees, or other large apes, in Borneo.

The grand saloon in which the masquerade was to take place was a circular room, very lofty, and receiving the light of the sun only through a single window at top. At night (the season for which the apartment was especially designed) it was illuminated principally by a large chandelier, depending by a chain from the center of the skylight, and lowered, or elevated, by means of a counterbalance as usual; but (in order not to look unsightly) this latter passed outside the cupola and over the roof.

The arrangements of the room had been

left to Trippetta's superintendence; but, in
some particulars, it seems, she had been
guided by the calmer judgment of her friend
the dwarf. At his suggestion it was that, on
this occasion, the chandelier was removed.
Its waxen drippings (which, in weather so
warm, it was quite impossible to prevent)
would have been seriously detrimental to the
rich dresses of the guests, who, on account
of the crowded state of the saloon, could not
all be expected to keep from out its center —
that is to say, from under the chandelier.
Additional sconces were set in various parts
of the hall, out of the way; and a flambeaux,
emitting sweet odor, was placed in the right
hand of each of the Caryatides that stood
against the wall — some fifty or sixty all
together.

The eight orangutans, taking Hop-Frog's
advice, waited patiently until midnight
(when the room was thoroughly filled with
masqueraders) before making their appearance. No sooner had the clock ceased striking, however, than they rushed, or rather
rolled in, all together — for the impediments
of their chains caused most of the party to
fall, and all to stumble as they entered.

The excitement among the masqueraders was prodigious, and filled the heart of the king with glee. As had been anticipated, there were not a few of the guests who supposed the ferocious-looking creatures to be beasts of *some* kind in reality, if not precisely orangutans. Many of the women swooned with affright; and had not the king taken the precaution to exclude all weapons from the saloon, his party might soon have expiated their frolic in their blood. As it was, a general rush was made for the doors; but the king had ordered them to be locked immediately upon his entrance; and, at the dwarf's suggestion, the keys had been deposited with *him*.

While the tumult was at its height, and each masquerader attentive only to his own safety (for, in fact, there was much *real* danger from the pressure of the excited crowd), the chain by which the chandelier ordinarily hung, and which had been drawn up on its removal, might have been seen very gradually to descend, until its hooked extremity came within three feet of the floor.

Soon after this, the king and his seven friends having reeled about the hall in all directions, found themselves, at length, in its center, and, of course, in immediate contact with the chain. While they were thus situated, the dwarf, who had followed noiselessly at their heels, inciting them to keep up the commotion, took hold of their own chain at the intersection of the two portions which crossed the circle diametrically and at right angles. Here, with the rapidity of thought, he inserted the hook from which the chandelier had been wont to depend; and, in an instant, by some unseen agency, the chandelier chain was drawn so far upward as to take the hook out of reach, and, as an inevitable consequence, to drag the orangutans together in close connection, and face to face.

The masqueraders, by this time, had recovered, in some measure, from their alarm; and, beginning to regard the whole matter as a well-contrived pleasantry, set up a loud shout of laughter at the predicament of the apes.

"Leave them to *me*!" now screamed Hop-Frog, his shrill voice making itself easily heard through all the din. "Leave them to *me*. I fancy *I* know them. If I can only get a good look at them, *I* can soon tell who they are."

Here, scrambling over the heads of the crowd, he managed to get to the wall; when, seizing a flambeaux from one of the Caryatides, he returned, as he went, to the center of the room — leaped, with the agility of a monkey, upon the king's head — and thence clambered a few feet up the chain — holding down the torch to examine the group of orangutans, and still screaming, "*I* shall soon find out who they are!"

And now, while the whole assembly (the apes included) were convulsed with laughter, the jester suddenly uttered a shrill whistle; when the chain flew violently up for about thirty feet — dragging with it the dismayed and struggling orangutans, and leaving them suspended in midair between the skylight and the floor. Hop-Frog, clinging to the chain as it rose, still maintained his relative position in respect to the eight maskers, and still (as if nothing were the matter) continued to thrust his torch down toward them, as though endeavoring to discover who they were.

So thoroughly astonished was the whole company at this ascent, that a dead silence, of about a minute's duration, ensued. It was broken by just such a low, harsh, *grating*

sound, as had before attracted the attention
of the king and his councilors when the former threw the wine in the face of Trippetta.
But, on the present occasion, there could be
no question as to *whence* the sound issued.
It came from the fanglike teeth of the dwarf,
who ground them and gnashed them as he
foamed at the mouth, and glared, with an
expression of maniacal rage, into the up-
turned countenances of the king and his
seven companions.

"Ah, ha!" said at length the infuriated
jester. "Ah, ha! I begin to see who these
people *are*, now!" Here, pretending to scru-
tinize the king more closely, he held the
flambeaux to the flaxen coat which enveloped
him, and which instantly burst into a sheet
of vivid flame. In less than half a minute the
whole eight orangutans were blazing fiercely,
amid the shrieks of the multitude who gazed
at them from below, horror-stricken, and
without the power to render them the slightest assistance.

At length the flames, suddenly increasing
in virulence, forced the jester to climb higher
up the chain, to be out of their reach; and,
as he made this movement, the crowd again
sank, for a brief instant, into silence. The

dwarf seized his opportunity, and once more spoke:

"I now see *distinctly*," he said, "what manner of people these maskers are. They are a great king and his seven privy councilors — a king who does not scruple to strike a defenseless girl, and his seven councilors who abet him in the outrage. As for myself, I am simply Hop-Frog, the jester — and *this is my last jest*."

Owing to the high combustibility of both the flax and the tar to which it adhered, the dwarf had scarcely made an end of his brief speech before the work of vengeance was complete. The eight corpses swung in their chains, a fetid, blackened, hideous, and indistinguishable mass. The cripple hurled his torch at them, clambered leisurely to the ceiling, and disappeared through the skylight.

It is supposed that Trippetta, stationed on the roof of the saloon, had been the accomplice of her friend in his fiery revenge, and that, together, they effected their escape to their own country; for neither was seen again.

MS. Found in a Bottle

The "I" of this story is a scientist who hates superstition. Such a man would report only what actually happened, says Poe; he would not stretch the facts. The "facts," of course, are strange and wonderful; they add up to a gripping tale of terror.

In writing this weird story of a ghost ship, did Poe make use of Samuel Coleridge's "The Rime of the Ancient Mariner"? The gloss, or prose guide, that appears alongside this poem contains such phrases as "The ship driven by a storm toward the South Pole" and "The land of ice, and of fearful sounds where no living thing was to be seen." These and other passages keep alive the rumor that Poe was deeply impressed by Coleridge's ballad of death.

In 1833, Poe sent several stories, perhaps as many as sixteen, to the *Baltimore Saturday Visiter* as entries in a contest. "MS. Found in a Bottle" won the first prize — fifty dollars.

Qui n'a plus qu'un moment à vivre
N'a plus rien à dissimuler.
                    — *Quinault — Atys*

Of my country and of my family I
have little to say. Ill-usage and length of
years have driven me from the one and
estranged me from the other. Hereditary
wealth afforded me an education of no common order, and a contemplative turn of mind
enabled me to methodize the stories which
early study diligently garnered up. Beyond
all things, the works of the German moralists
gave me great delight; not from my ill-advised
admiration of their eloquent madness, but
from the ease with which my habits of rigid

thoughts enabled me to detect their falsities. I have often been reproached with the aridity of my genius; a deficiency of imagination has been imputed to me as a crime; and the Pyrrhonism of my opinions has at all times rendered me notorious. Indeed, a strong relish for physical philosophy has, I fear, tinctured my mind with a very common error of this age — I mean the habit of referring occurences, even the least susceptible of such reference, to the principles of that science. Upon the whole, no person could be less liable than myself to be led away from the severe precincts of truth by the *ignes fatui* of superstition. I have thought proper to premise thus much, lest the incredible tale I have to tell should be considered rather the raving of a crude imagination than the positive experience of a mind to which the reveries of fancy have been a dead letter and a nullity.

After many years spent in foreign travel, I sailed in the year 18— from the port of Batavia, in the rich and populous island of Java, on a voyage to the Archipelago Islands. I went as passenger, having no other inducement than a kind of nervous restlessness which haunted me as a fiend.

Our vessel was a beautiful ship of about four hundred tons, copper-fastened, and built at Bombay of Malabar teak. She was freighted with cotton wool and oil, from the Lachadive Islands. We had also on board coir, jaggeree, ghee, coconuts, and a few cases of opium. The stowage was clumsily done, and the vessel consequently crank.

We got underway with a mere breath of wind, and for many days stood along the eastern coast of Java, without any other incident to beguile the monotony of our course than the occasional meeting with some of the small grabs of the Archipelago to which we were bound.

One evening, leaning over the taffrail, I observed a very singular isolated cloud, to the NW. It was remarkable, as well from its color as from its being the first we had seen since our departure from Batavia. I watched it attentively until sunset, when it spread all at once to the eastward and westward, girting in the horizon with a narrow strip of vapor, and looking like a long line of low beach. My notice was soon afterward attracted by the dusky-red appearance of the moon and the peculiar character of the sea. The latter was undergoing a rapid change, and the water seemed more than usually transparent. Although I could distinctly see the bottom, yet, heaving the lead, I found the ship in fifteen fathoms. The air now became intolerably hot, and was loaded with spiral exhalations similar to those arising from heated iron. As night came on, every breath of wind died away, and a more entire calm it is impossible to conceive. The flame of a candle burned upon the poop without the least perceptible motion, and a long hair, held between the finger and thumb, hung without the possibility of detecting a vibration. However, as the captain said he could perceive no indication of danger, and as we were drifting in bodily to shore, he ordered the sails to be furled and the anchor let go. No watch was set, and the crew, consisting principally of Malays, stretched themselves deliberately upon deck. I went below — not without a full presentiment of evil. Indeed, every appearance warranted me in apprehending a simoon. I told the captain of my fears; but he paid no attention to what I said, and left me without deigning to give a reply. My uneasiness, however, prevented me from sleeping, and about midnight I went upon deck. As I placed my foot upon the upper step of the companion ladder, I was startled by a loud, humming noise, like that occasioned by the rapid revolution of a mill wheel, and before I could ascertain its meaning, I found the ship quivering to its center. In the next instant a wilderness of foam hurled up upon our beam ends, and, rushing over us fore and aft, swept the entire deck from stem to stern.

The extreme fury of the blast proved, in a great measure, the salvation of the ship. Although completely waterlogged, yet, as her masts had gone by the board, she rose, after a minute, heavily from the sea, and, staggering awhile beneath the immense pressure of the tempest, finally righted.

By what miracle I escaped destruction, it is impossible to say. Stunned by the shock of the water, I found myself, upon recovery, jammed in between the stern post and rudder. With great difficulty I regained my feet, and looking dizzily around, was at first struck with the idea of our being among breakers; so terrific, beyond the wildest imagination, was the whirlpool of mountainous and foaming ocean within which we were engulfed. After a while I heard the voice of an old

Swede, who had shipped with us at the moment of leaving port. I hallooed to him with all my strength, and presently he came reeling aft. We soon discovered that we were the sole survivors of the accident. All on deck, with the exception of ourselves, had been swept overboard; the captain and mates must have perished while they slept, for the cabins were deluged with water. Without assistance we could expect to do little for the security of the ship, and our exertions were at first paralyzed by the momentary expectation of going down. Our cable had, of course, parted like pack thread, at the first breath of the hurricane, or we should have been instantaneously overwhelmed. We scudded with frightful velocity before the sea, and the water made clear breaches over us. The framework of our stern was shattered excessively, and, in almost every respect, we had received considerable injury; but to our extreme joy we found the pumps unchocked, and that we had made no great shifting of our ballast. The main fury of the blast had already blown over, and we apprehended little danger from the violence of the wind; but we looked forward to its total cessation with dismay, well believing that, in our shattered condition, we should inevitably perish in the tremendous swell which would ensue. But this very just apprehension seemed by no means likely to be soon verified. For five entire days and nights — during which our only subsistence was a small quantity of jaggeree, procured with great difficulty from the forecastle — the hulk flew at a rate defying computation, before rapidly succeeding flaws of wind, which, without equaling the first violence of the simoon, were still more terrific than any tempest I had before encountered. Our course for the first four days was, with trifling variations, SE and by S; and we must have run down the coast of New Holland. On the fifth day the cold became extreme, although the wind had hauled round a point more to the northward. The sun arose with a sickly yellow luster, and clambered a very few degrees above the horizon, emitting no decisive light. There were no clouds apparent, yet the wind was upon the increase, and blew with a fitful and unsteady fury. About noon, as nearly as we could guess, our attention was again arrested by the appearance of the sun. It gave out no light, properly so called, but a dull and sullen glow without reflection, as if all its rays were polarized. Just before sinking within the turgid sea, its central fires suddenly went out, as if hurriedly extinguished by some unaccountable power. It was a dim, silver-like rim, alone, as it rushed down the unfathomable ocean.

We waited in vain for the arrival of the sixth day — that day to me has not yet arrived — to the Swede never did arrive. Thenceforward we were enshrouded in pitchy darkness, so that we could not have seen an object at twenty paces from the ship. Eternal night continued to envelop us, all unrelieved by the phosphoric sea brilliancy to which we had been accustomed in the tropics. We observed, too, that, although the tempest continued to rage with unabated violence, there was no longer to be discovered the usual appearance of surf, or foam, which had hitherto attended us. All around were horror, and thick gloom, and a black sweltering desert of ebony. Superstitious terror crept by degrees into the spirit of the old Swede, and my own soul was wrapt in silent wonder. We neglected all care of the ship, as worse than useless, and securing ourselves as well as possible to the stump of the mizenmast, looked out bitterly into the world of ocean. We had no means of calculating time, nor could we form any guess of our situation. We were, however, well aware of having made farther to the southward than any previous navigators, and felt great amazement at not meeting with the usual impediments of ice. In the meantime every moment threatened to be our last — every mountainous billow hurried to overwhelm us. The swell surpassed anything I had imagined possible, and that we were not instantly buried is a miracle. My companion spoke of the lightness of our cargo, and reminded me of the excellent qualities of our ship; but I could not help feeling the utter hopelessness of hope itself, and prepared myself gloomily for that death which I thought nothing could defer beyond an hour, as, with every knot of way the ship made, the swelling of the black stupendous seas became more dismally appalling. At times we gasped for breath at an elevation beyond the albatross—at times became dizzy with the velocity of our descent into some watery hell, where the air grew stagnant, and no sound disturbed the slumbers of the kraken.

We were at the bottom of one of these

abysses when a quick scream from my companion broke fearfully upon the night. "See! see!" cried he, shrieking in my ears, "Almighty God! see! see!" As he spoke, I became aware of a dull sullen glare of red light which streamed down the sides of the vast chasm where we lay and threw a fitful brilliancy upon our deck. Casting my eyes upwards, I beheld a spectacle which froze the current of my blood. At a terrific height directly above us, and upon the very verge of the precipitous descent, hovered a gigantic ship of perhaps four thousand tons. Although upreared upon the summit of a wave more than a hundred times her own altitude, her apparent size still exceeded that of any ship of the line or East Indianman in existence. Her huge hull was of a deep dingy black, unrelieved by any of the customary carvings of a ship. A single row of brass cannon protruded from her open ports, and dashed from the polished surface the first of innumerable battle lanterns which swung to and fro about her rigging. But what mainly inspired us with horror and astonishment was that she bore up under a press of sail in the very teeth of that supernatural sea and of that

ungovernable hurricane. When we first discovered her, her bows were alone to be seen,
as she rose slowly from the dim and horrible
gulf beyond her. For a moment of intense
terror she paused upon the giddy pinnacle, as
if in contemplation of her own sublimity,
then trembled and tottered, and — came
down.

At this instant, I know not what sudden
self-possession came over my spirit. Staggering as far aft as I could, I awaited fearlessly
the ruin that was to overwhelm. Our own
vessel was at length ceasing from her struggles, and sinking with her head to the sea.
The shock of the descending mass struck her,
consequently, in that portion of her frame
which was nearly under water, and the inevitable result was to hurl me, with irresistible
violence, upon the rigging of the stranger.

As I fell, the ship hove in stays and went
about; and to the confusion ensuing I attributed my escape from the notice of the
crew. With little difficulty I made my way,
unperceived, to the main hatchway, which
was partially open, and soon found an opportunity of secreting myself in the hold.
Why I did so I can hardly tell. An indefinite

sense of awe, which at first sight of the navigators of the ship had taken hold of my mind, was perhaps the principle of my concealment. I was unwilling to trust myself with a race of people who had offered, to the cursory glance I had taken, so many points of vague novelty, doubt, and apprehension. I therefore thought proper to contrive a hiding place in the hold. This I did by removing a small portion of the shifting boards, in such a manner as to afford me a convenient retreat between the huge timbers of the ship.

I had scarcely completed my work when a footstep in the hold forced me to make use of it. A man passed by my place of concealment with a feeble and unsteady gait. I could not see his face, but had an opportunity of observing his general appearance. There was about it an evidence of great age and infirmity. His knees tottered beneath a load of years, and his entire frame quivered under the burden. He muttered to himself, in a low broken tone, some words of a language which I could not understand, and groped in a corner among a pile of singular-looking instruments and decayed charts of navigation. His manner was a wild mixture of the peevishness of second childhood, and the solemn dignity of a God. He at length went on deck, and I saw him no more.

A feeling, for which I have no name, has taken possession of my soul — a sensation which will admit of no analysis, to which the lessons of bygone time are inadequate, and for which I fear futurity itself will offer me no key. To a mind constituted like my own, the latter consideration is an evil. I shall never — I know that I shall never — be satisfied with regard to the nature of my conceptions. Yet it is not wonderful that these conceptions are indefinite, since they have their origin in sources so utterly novel. A new sense — a new entity is added to my soul.

It is long since I first trod the deck of this terrible ship, and the rays of my destiny are, I think, gathering to a focus. Incomprehensible men! Wrapped up in meditations of a kind which I cannot divine, they pass me by unnoticed. Concealment is utter folly on my part, for the people *will not* see. It is but just now that I passed directly before the eyes of the mate; it was no long while ago that I ventured into the captain's own private cabin, and took thence the materials with which I write and have written. I shall from time to time continue this journal. It is true that I may not find an opportunity of transmitting it to the world, but I will not fail to make the endeavor. At the last moment I will enclose the MS. in a bottle and cast it within the sea.

An incident has occurred which has given me new room for meditation. Are such things the operation of ungoverned chance? I had ventured upon deck and thrown myself down, without attracting any notice, among a pile of ratlin stuff and old sails, in the bottom of the yawl. While musing upon the singularity of my fate, I unwittingly daubed with a tar brush the edges of a neatly folded studding sail which lay near me on a barrel. The studding sail is now bent upon the ship, and the thoughtless touches of the brush are spread out into the word DISCOVERY.

I have made my observations lately upon the structure of the vessel. Although well armed, she is not, I think, a ship of war. Her rigging, build, and general equipment, all negative a supposition of this kind. What she *is not*, I can easily perceive; what she *is*, I fear it is impossible to say. I know not how it is, but in scrutinizing her strange model and singular cast of spars, her huge size and overgrown suits of canvas, her severely simple bow and antiquated stern, there will occasionally flash across my mind a sensation of familiar things, and there is always mixed up with such indistinct shadows of recollection, an unaccountable memory of old foreign chronicles and ages long ago.

I have been looking at the timbers of the ship. She is built of a material to which I am a stranger. There is a peculiar character about the wood which strikes me as rendering it unfit for the purpose to which it has been applied. I mean its extreme *porousness*, considered independently of the worm-eaten condition which is a consequence of navigation in these seas, and apart from the rottenness attendant upon age. It will appear perhaps an observation somewhat overcurious, but this would have every characteristic of Spanish oak, if Spanish oak were distended by any unnatural means.

In reading the above sentence, a curious

apothegm of an old weather-beaten Dutch navigator comes full upon my recollection. "It is as sure," he was wont to say, when any doubt was entertained of his veracity, "as sure as there is a sea where the ship itself will grow in bulk like the living body of the seaman."

About an hour ago, I made bold to thrust myself among a group of the crew. They paid me no manner of attention, and, although I stood in the very midst of them all, seemed utterly unconscious of my presence. Like the one I had at first seen in the hold, they all bore about them the marks of a hoary old age. Their knees trembled with infirmity; their shoulders were bent double with decrepitude; their shriveled skins rattled in the wind; their voices were low, tremulous, and broken; their eyes glistened with the rheum of years; and their gray hairs streamed terribly in the tempest. Around them, on every part of the deck, lay scattered mathematical instruments of the most quaint and obsolete construction.

I mentioned some time ago, the bending of a studding sail. From that period, the ship, being thrown dead off the wind, has continued her terrific course due south, with every rag of canvas packed upon her, from her truck to her lower studding-sail booms, and rolling every moment her top-gallant yardarms into the most appalling hell of water which it can enter into the mind of man to imagine. I have just left the deck, where I find it impossible to maintain a footing, although the crew seem to experience little inconvenience. It appears to me a miracle of miracles that our enormous bulk is not swallowed up at once and forever. We are surely doomed to hover continually upon the brink of eternity, without taking a final plunge into the abyss. From billows a thousand times more stupendous than any I have ever seen, we glide away with the facility of the arrowy sea gull; and the colossal waters rear their heads above us like demons of the deep, but like demons confined to simple threats, and forbidden to destroy. I am led to attribute these frequent escapes to the only natural cause which can account for such effect. I must suppose the ship to be within the influence of some strong current, or impetuous undertow.

* * *

I have seen the captain face to face, and
in his own cabin — but, as I expected, he
paid me no attention. Although in his appearance there is, to a casual observer, nothing which might bespeak him more or less
than man, still, a feeling of irrepressible rev-
erence and awe mingled with the sensation
of wonder with which I regarded him. In
stature, he is nearly my own height; that is,
about five feet eight inches. He is of a well-
knit and compact frame of body, neither
robust nor remarkable otherwise. But it is
the singularity of the expression which
reigns upon the face — it is the intense, the
wonderful, the thrilling evidence of old age
so utter, so extreme, which excites within
my spirit a sense — a sentiment ineffable.
His forehead, although little wrinkled, seems
to bear upon it the stamp of a myriad of
years. His gray hairs are records of the past,
and his grayer eyes are sybils of the future.
The cabin floor was thickly strewn with
strange, iron-clasped folios, and moldering
instruments of science, and obsolete long-
forgotten charts. His head was bowed down
upon his hands, and he pored, with a fiery,

unquiet eye, over a paper which I took to be a commission, and which, at all events, bore the signature of a monarch. He murmured to himself — as did the first seaman whom I saw in the hold — some low peevish syllables of a foreign tongue; and although the speaker was close at my elbow, his voice seemed to reach my ears from the distance of a mile.

The ship and all in it are imbued with the spirit of Eld. The crew glide to and fro like the ghosts of buried centuries; their eyes have an eager and uneasy meaning; and when their fingers fall athwart my path in the wild glare of the battle lanterns, I feel as I have never felt before, although I have been all my life a dealer in antiquities, and have imbibed the shadows of fallen columns at Balbec, and Tadmor, and Persepolis, until my very soul has become a ruin.

When I look around me, I feel ashamed of my former apprehension. If I trembled at the blast which has hitherto attended us, shall I not stand aghast at a warring of wind and ocean, to convey any idea of which, the words tornado and simoon are trivial and ineffective? All in the immediate vicinity of the ship is the blackness of eternal night, and a chaos of foamless water; but, about a league on either side of us, may be seen, indistinctly and at intervals, stupendous ramparts of ice, towering away into the desolate sky, and looking like the walls of the universe.

As I imagined, the ship proves to be in a current — if that appellation can properly be given to a tide which, howling and shrieking by the white ice, thunders on the southward with a velocity like the headlong dashing of a cataract.

To conceive the horror of my sensations is, I presume, utterly impossible; yet a curiosity to penetrate the mysteries of these awful regions predominates even over my despair, and will reconcile me to the most hideous aspect of death. It is evident that we are hurrying onward to some exciting knowledge — some never-to-be-imparted secret, whose attainment is destruction. Perhaps this current leads us to the southern pole itself. It must be confessed that a supposition apparently so wild has every probability in its favor.

The crew pace the deck with unquiet and

tremulous step; but there is upon their countenance an expression more of the eagerness
of hope than of the apathy of despair.

In the meantime the wind is still in our
poop, and, as we carry a crowd of canvas, the
ship is at times lifted bodily from out the
sea! Oh, horror upon horror! — the ice opens
suddenly to the right, and to the left, and we
are whirling dizzily, in immense concentric
circles, round and round the borders of a
gigantic amphitheatre, the summit of whose
walls is lost in the darkness and the distance.
But little time will be left me to ponder upon
my destiny! The circles rapidly grow small —
we are plunging madly within the grasp of
the whirlpool — and amid a roaring, and bel-
lowing, and thundering of ocean and tempest,
the ship is quivering — oh God! and — going
down!

Note: The "MS. Found in a Bottle," was originally
published in 1831, and it was not until many years
afterward that I became acquainted with the maps
of Mercator, in which the ocean is represented as
rushing, by four mouths, into the (northern) Polar
Gulf, to be absorbed into the bowels of the earth;
the Pole itself being represented by a black rock,
towering to a prodigious height.

Ligeia

Poe received ten dollars for this superb reincarnation story which was first published in the Baltimore *American Museum* for September, 1838. Ligeia, the dark lady of the Rhineland, wastes away and dies, but her spirit triumphs over death and follows her grieving husband to England. Here he takes a second wife, the blond Lady Rowena, but his soul is still mated to the bewitching Ligeia. In great agony of longing for the lost Ligeia, he does not think it strange that his second wife is "attacked with sudden illness" about a month after their marriage, but at the subsequent death of the Lady Rowena he has a surprise in store for him. Ligeia takes possession of the corpse, transforming it into a physical image of herself. As her beloved husband looks on in horror, she rises from Lady Rowena's deathbed, lets fall her long black hair, and slowly opens her large and luminous eyes. He can only *shriek* his recognition.

Poe was not happy about this ending and wrote: "I should have intimated that the *will* did not perfect its intention. There should have been a relapse — a final one — and Ligeia should be at length entombed as Rowena, the bodily alterations having gradually faded away."

And the will therein lieth, which dieth not. Who
knoweth the mysteries of the will, with its vigor?
For God is but a great will pervading all things
by nature of its intentness. Man doth not yield
himself to the angels, nor unto death utterly,
save only through the weakness of his feeble will.
— *Joseph Glanvill*

I cannot, for my soul, remember how,
when, or even precisely where I first became
acquainted with the Lady Ligeia. Long years
have since elapsed, and my memory is feeble
through much suffering. Or, perhaps, I cannot *now* bring these points to mind, because,
in truth, the character of my beloved, her
rare learning, her singular yet placid cast of

beauty, and the thrilling and enthralling eloquence of her low musical language, made their way into my heart by paces so steadily and stealthily progressive that they have been unnoticed and unknown. Yet I believe that I met her first and most frequently in some large, old, decaying city near the Rhine. Of her family — I have surely heard her speak. That it is of a remotely ancient date cannot be doubted. Ligeia! Ligeia! Buried in studies of a nature more than all else adapted to deaden impressions of the outward world, it is by that sweet word alone — by Ligeia — that I bring before mine eyes in fancy the image of her who is no more. And now, while I write, a recollection flashes upon me that I have *never known* the paternal name of her who was my friend and my betrothed, and who became the partner of my studies, and finally the wife of my bosom. Was it a playful charge on the part of my Ligeia? or was it a test of my strength of affection that I should institute no inquiries upon this point? or was it rather a caprice of my own — a wildly romantic offering on the shrine of the most passionate devotion? I but indistinctly recall the fact itself — what wonder that I

have utterly forgotten the circumstances
which originated or attended it? And, indeed,
if ever that spirit which is entitled *Romance*
— if ever she, the wan and the mistywinged
Ashtophet of idolatrous Egypt, presided, as
they tell, over marriages ill-omened, then
most surely she presided over mine.

There is one dear topic, however, on which
my memory fails me not. It is the *person* of
Ligeia. In stature she was tall, somewhat
slender, and, in her latter days, even emaciated. I would in vain attempt to portray the
majesty, the quiet ease of her demeanor, or
the incomprehensible lightness and elasticity
of her footfall. She came and departed as a
shadow. I was never made aware of her entrance into my closed study, save by the dear
music of her low, sweet voice, as she placed
her marble hand upon my shoulder. In beauty
of face no maiden ever equaled her. It was
the radiance of an opium dream — an airy
and spiritlifting vision more wildly divine
than the phantasies which hovered about the
slumbering souls of the daughters of Delos.
Yet her features were not of that regular
mold which we have been falsely taught to
worship in the classical labors of the

heathen. "There is no exquisite beauty," says
Bacon, Lord Verulam, speaking truly of all
the forms and *genera* of beauty, "without
some *strangeness* in the proportion." Yet,
although I saw that the features of Ligeia
were not of a classic regularity — although
I perceived that her loveliness was indeed
"exquisite," and felt that there was much of
"strangeness" pervading it, yet I have tried
in vain to detect the irregularity and to trace
home my own perception of "the strange." I
examined the contour of the lofty and pale
forehead — it was faultless — how cold indeed that word when applied to a majesty so
divine! — the skin rivaling the purest ivory,
the commanding extent and repose, the gentle
prominence of the regions above the temples;
and then the raven-black, the glossy, the
luxuriant, and naturally curling tresses, setting forth the full force of the Homeric
epithet, "hyacinthine!" I looked at the delicate outlines of the nose — and nowhere but
in the graceful medallions of the Hebrews
had I beheld a similar perfection. There were
the same luxurious smoothness of surface, the
same scarcely perceptible tendency to the
aquiline, the same harmoniously curved nos-

trils speaking the free spirit. I regarded the sweet mouth. Here was indeed the triumph of all things heavenly — the magnificent turn of the short upper lip — the soft, voluptuous slumber of the under — the dimples which sported, and the color which spoke — the teeth glancing back, with a brilliancy almost startling, every ray of the holy light which fell upon them in her serene and placid yet most exultingly radiant of all smiles. I scrutinized the formation of the chin — and, here too, I found the gentleness of breadth, the softness and the majesty, the fullness and the spirituality, of the Greek — the contour which the god Apollo revealed but in a dream, to Cleomenes, the son of the Athenian. And then I peered into the large eyes of Ligeia.

For eyes we have no models in the remotely antique. It might have been, too, that in these eyes of my beloved lay the secret to which Lord Verulam alludes. They were, I must believe, far larger than the ordinary eyes of our own race. They were even fuller than the fullest of the gazelle eyes of the tribe of the valley of Nourjahad. Yet it was only at intervals — in moments of intense excitement

— that this pecularity became more than
slightly noticeable in Ligeia. And at such moments was her beauty — in my heated fancy
thus it appeared perhaps — the beauty of
beings either above or apart from the earth
— the beauty of the fabulous Houri of the
Turk. The hue of the orbs was the most
brilliant of black, and, far over them, hung
jetty lashes of great length. The brows,
slightly irregular in outline, had the same
tint. The "strangeness," however, which I
found in the eyes was of a nature distinct
from the formation, or the color, or the
brilliancy of the features, and must, after all,
be referred to the *expression*. Ah, word of no
meaning! behind whose vast latitude of mere
sound we entrench our ignorance of so much
of the spiritual. The expression of the eyes
of Ligeia! How for long hours have I pondered upon it! How have I, through the whole
of a midsummer night, struggled to fathom
it! What was it — that something more profound than the well of Democritus — which
lay far within the pupils of my beloved?
What *was* it? I was possessed with a passion
to discover. Those eyes! those large, those
shining, those divine orbs! they became to

me twin stars of Leda, and I to them devoutest of astrologers.

There is no point, among the may incomprehensible anomalies of the science of mind, more thrillingly exciting than the fact — never, I believe, noticed in the schools — that in our endeavors to recall to memory something long forgotten, we often find ourselves *upon the very verge* of remembrance, without being able, in the end, to remember. And thus how frequently, in my intense scrutiny of Ligeia's eyes, have I felt approaching the full knowledge of their expression — felt it approaching — yet not quite be mine — and so at length entirely depart! And (strange, oh, strangest mystery of all!) I found, in the commonest objects of the universe, a circle of analogies to that expression. I mean to say that, subsequently to the period when Ligeia's beauty passed into my spirit, there dwelling as in a shrine, I derived, from many existences in the material world, a sentiment such as I felt always around, within me, by her large and luminous orbs. Yet not the more could I define that sentiment, or analyze, or even steadily view it. I recognized it, let me repeat, sometimes in the survey of

a rapidly growing vine — in the contemplation of a moth, a butterfly, a chrysalis, a
stream of running water. I have felt it in the
ocean — in the falling of a meteor. I have
felt it in the glances of unusually aged people.
And there are one or two stars in heaven
(one especially, a star of the sixth magni-
tude, double and changeable, to be found
near the large star in Lyra) in a telescopic
scrutiny of which I have been made aware of
the feeling. I have been filled with it by certain sounds from stringed instruments, and
not unfrequently by passages from books.
Among innumerable other instances, I well
remember something in a volume of Joseph
Glanvill, which (perhaps merely from its
quaintness — who shall say?) never failed
to inspire me with the sentiment: "And the
will therein lieth, which dieth not. Who
knoweth the mysteries of the will, with its
vigor? For God is but a great will pervading
all things by nature of its intentness. Man
doth not yield him to the angels, nor unto
death utterly, save only through the weakness of his feeble will."

Length of years and subsequent reflection
have enabled me to trace, indeed, some re-

mote connection between this passage in the English moralist and a portion of the character of Ligeia. An *intensity* in thought, action, or speech was possibly, in her, a result, or at least an index, of that gigantic volition which, during our long intercourse, failed to give other and more immediate evidence of its existence. Of all the women whom I have ever known, she, the outwardly calm, the ever-placid Ligeia, was the most violently a prey to the tumultuous vultures of stern passion. And of such passion I could form no estimate, save by the miraculous expansion of those eyes which at once so delighted and appalled me — by the almost magical melody, modulation, distinctness, and placidity of her very low voice — and by the fierce energy (rendered doubly effective by contrast with her manner of utterance) of the wild words which she habitually uttered.

I have spoken of the learning of Ligeia: it was immense — such as I have never known in woman. In the classical tongues was she deeply proficient, and as far as my own acquaintance extended in regard to the modern dialects of Europe, I have never known her

at fault. Indeed upon any theme of the most
admired, because simply the most abstruse of
the boasted erudition of the Academy, have
I *ever* found Ligeia at fault? How singularly
— how thrillingly, this one point in the nature of my wife has forced itself, at this late
period only, upon my attention! I said her
knowledge was such as I have never known
in woman — but where breathes the man who
has traversed, and successfully, *all* the wide
areas of moral, physical, and mathematical
science? I saw not then what I now clearly
perceive, that the acquisitions of Ligeia were
gigantic, were astounding; yet I was sufficiently aware of her infinite supremacy to
resign myself, with a childlike confidence, to
her guidance through the chaotic world of
metaphysical investigation at which I was
most busily occupied during the earlier years
of our marriage. With how vast a triumph —
with how vivid a delight — with how much
of all that is ethereal in hope did I *feel*, as
she bent over me in studies but little sought,
but less known — that delicious vista by slow
degrees expanding before me, down whose
long, gorgeous, and all untrodden path I

might at length pass onward to the goal of a wisdom too divinely precious not to be forbidden!

How poignant, then, must have been the grief with which, after some years, I beheld my well-grounded expectations take wings to themselves and fly away! Without Ligeia I was but as a child groping benighted. Her presence, her readings alone, rendered vividly luminous the many mysteries of the transcendentalism in which we were immersed. Wanting the radiant luster of her eyes, letters, lambent and golden, grew duller than Saturnian lead. And now those eyes shone less and less frequently upon the pages over which I pored. Ligeia grew ill. The wild eyes blazed with a too — too glorious effulgence; the pale fingers became of the transparent waxen hue of the grave; and the blue veins upon the lofty forehead swelled and sank impetuously with the tides of the most gentle emotion. I saw that she must die — and I struggled desperately in spirit with the grim Azrael. And the struggles of the passionate wife were, to my astonishment, even more energetic than my own. There had been much

in her stern nature to impress me with the
belief that, to her, death would have come
without its terrors; but not so. Words are
impotent to convey any just idea of the fierceness of resistance with which she wrestled
with the Shadow. I groaned in anguish at the
pitiable spectacle. I would have soothed — I
would have reasoned; but in the intensity of
her wild desire for life — for life — *but* for
life — solace and reason were alike the utter-
most of folly. Yet not until the last instance,
amid the most convulsive writhings of her
fierce spirit, was shaken the external placidity of her demeanor. Her voice grew more
gentle — grew more low — yet I would not
wish to dwell upon the wild meaning of the
quietly uttered words. My brain reeled as I
hearkened, entranced to a melody more than
mortal — to assumptions and aspirations
which mortality had never before known.

That she loved me I should not have
doubted; and I might have been easily aware
that, in a bosom such as hers, love would
have reigned no ordinary passion. But in
death only was I fully impressed with the
strength of her affection. For long hours,

detaining my hand, would she pour out before
me the overflowing of a heart whose more
than passionate devotion amounted to idol-
atry. How had I deserved to be so blessed by
such confessions? — how had I deserved to
be so cursed with the removal of my beloved
in the hour of my making them? But upon
this subject I cannot bear to dilate. Let me
say only that, in Ligeia's more than womanly
abandonment to a love, alas! all unmerited,
all unworthily bestowed, I at length recognized the principle of her longing, with so
wildly earnest a desire, for the life which
was now fleeing so rapidly away. It is this
wild longing — it is this eager vehemence
of desire for life—*but* for life — that I have
no power to portray — no utterance capable
of expressing.

At high noon of the night in which she
departed, beckoning me, peremptorily, to her
side, she bade me repeat certain verses composed by herself not many days before. I
obeyed her. They were these:

Lo! 'tis a gala night
    Within the lonesome latter years!
An angel throng, bewinged, bedight
    In veils, and drowned in tears,

Sit in a theater, to see
   A play of hopes and fears,
While the orchestra breathes fitfully
   The music of the spheres.

Mimes, in the form of God on high,
   Mutter and mumble low,
And hither and thither fly —
   Mere puppets they, who come and go
At bidding of vast formless things
   That shift the scenery to and fro,
Flapping from out their Condor wings
   Invisible Wo!

That motley drama! — oh, be sure
   It shall not be forgot!
With its Phantom chased forever more,
   By a crowd that seize it not,
Through a circle that ever returneth in
   To the self-same spot,
And much of Madness and more of Sin
   And Horror the soul of the plot.

But see, amid the mimic rout,
   A crawling shape intrude!
A blood-red thing that writhes from out
   The scenic solitude!
It writhes! — it writhes! — with mortal pangs
   The mimes become its food,
And the seraphs sob at vermin fangs
   In human gore imbued.

Out — out are the lights — out all!
  And over each quivering form,
The curtain, a funeral pall,
  Comes down with the rush of a storm,
And the angels, all pallid and wan,
  Uprising, unveiling, affirm
That the play is the tragedy, "Man,"
  And its hero the Conqueror Worm.

"O God!" half shrieked Ligeia, leaping to her feet and extending her arms aloft with a spasmodic movement, as I made an end of these lines — "Oh God! O Divine Father! — shall these things be undeviatingly so? — shall this conqueror be not once conquered? Are we not part and parcel in Thee? Who — who knoweth the mysteries of the will with its vigor? Man doth not yield him to the angels, *nor unto death utterly*, save only through the weakness of his feeble will."

And now, as if exhausted with emotion, she suffered her white arms to fall, and returned solemnly to her bed of death. And as she breathed her last sighs, there came mingled with them a low murmur from her lips. I bent to them my ear, and distinguished, again, the concluding words of the passage in Glanvill: *"Man doth not yield*

*him to the angels, nor unto death utterly,
save only through the weakness of his feeble
will.*"

She died: and I, crushed into the very dust
with sorrow, could no longer endure the
lonely desolation of my dwelling in the dim
and decaying city by the Rhine. I had no lack
of what the world calls wealth. Ligeia had
brought me far more, very far more, than
ordinarily falls to the lot of mortals. After a
few months, therefore, of weary and aimless
wandering, I purchased and put in some re-
pair, an abbey, which I shall not name, in one
of the wildest and least frequented portions
of fair England. The gloomy and dreary
grandeur of the building, the almost savage
aspect of the domain, the many melancholy
and time-honored memories connected with
both, had much in unison with the feelings
of utter abandonment which had driven me
into that remote and unsocial region of the
country. Yet although the external abbey,
with its verdant decay hanging about it, suffered but little alteration, I gave way, with
a childlike perversity, and perchance with a
faint hope of alleviating my sorrows, to a
display of more than regal magnificence

within. For such follies, even in childhood,
I had imbibed a taste, and now they came
back to me as if in the dotage of grief. Alas,
I feel how much even of incipient madness
might have been discovered in the gorgeous
and fantastic draperies, in the solemn carvings of Egypt, in the wild cornices and furniture, in the Bedlam patterns of the carpets
of tufted gold! I had become a bounden slave
in the trammels of opium, and my labors
and my orders had taken a coloring from my
dreams. But these absurdities I must not
pause to detail. Let me speak only of that one
chamber, ever accursed, whither, in a moment of mental alienation, I led from the
altar as my bride — as the successor of the
unforgotten Ligeia — the fair-haired and
blue-eyed Lady Rowena Trevanion, of Tremaine.

There is no individual portion of the archi-
tecture and decoration of that bridal chamber which is not now visibly before me.
Where were the souls of the haughty family
of the bride, when, through thirst of gold,
they permitted to pass the threshold of an
apartment *so* bedecked, a maiden and a
daughter so beloved? I have said that I

minutely remember the details of the chamber — yet I am sadly forgetful on topics of
deep moment; and here there was no system,
no keeping, in the fantastic display, to take
hold upon the memory. The room lay in a
high turret of the castellated abbey, was
pentagonal in shape, and of capacious size.
Occupying the whole southern face of the
pentagon was the sole window — an immense
sheet of unbroken glass from Venice — a
single pane, and tinted of a leaden hue, so
that the rays of either the sun or moon passing through it fell with a ghastly luster on
the objects within. Over the upper portion of
this huge window extended the trelliswork
of an aged vine, which clambered up the
massy walls of the turret. The ceiling, of
gloomy-looking oak, was excessively lofty,
vaulted, and elaborately fretted with the
wildest and most grotesque specimens of a
semi-Gothic, semi-Druidical device. From out
the most central recess of this melancholy
vaulting depended, by a single chain of gold
with long links, a huge censer of the same
metal, Saracenic in pattern, and with many
perforations so contrived that there writhed
in and out of them, as if endued with a ser-

pent vitality, a continual succession of particolored fires.

Some few ottomans and golden candelabra,
of Eastern figure, were in various stations
about; and there was the couch, too — the
bridal couch — of an Indian model, and low,
and sculptured of solid ebony, with a pall-like
canopy above. In each of the angles of the
chamber stood on end a gigantic sarcophagus
of black granite, from the tombs of the kings
over against Luxor, with their aged lids full
of immemorial sculpture. But in the draping
of the apartment lay, alas! the chief phantasy
of all. The lofty walls, gigantic in height —
even unproportionably so — were hung from
summit to foot, in vast folds, with a heavy
and massive-looking tapestry — tapestry of
a material which was found alike as a carpet
on the floor, as a covering for the ottomans
and the ebony bed, as a canopy for the bed
and as the gorgeous volutes of the curtains
which partially shaded the window. The material was the richest cloth of gold. It was
spotted all over, at irregular intervals, with
arabesque figures, about a foot in diameter,
and wrought upon the cloth in patterns of
the most jetty black. But these figures par-

took of the true character of the arabesque
only when regarded from a single point of
view. By a contrivance now common, and indeed traceable to a very remote period of
antiquity, they were made changeable in
aspect. To one entering the room, they bore
the appearance of simple monstrosities; but
upon a farther advance, this appearance
gradually departed; and, step by step, as the
visitor moved his station in the chamber, he
saw himself surrounded by an endless succession of the ghastly forms which belong to
the superstition of the Norman, or arise in
the guilty slumbers of the monk. The phantasmagoric effect was vastly heightened by
the artificial introduction of a strong continual current of wind behind the draperies
— giving a hideous and uneasy animation
to the whole.

In halls such as these — in a bridal chamber such as this — I passed, with the Lady of
Tremaine, the unhallowed hours of the first
month of our marriage — passed them with
but little disquietude. That my wife dreaded
the fierce moodiness of my temper — that
she shunned me, and loved me but little — I
could not help perceiving; but it gave me

rather pleasure than otherwise. I loathed her with a hatred belonging more to demon than to man. My memory flew back (oh, with what intensity of regret!) to Ligeia, the beloved, the august, the beautiful, the entombed. I reveled in recollections of her purity, of her wisdom, of her lofty — her ethereal nature, of her passionate, her idolatrous love. Now, then, did my spirit fully and freely burn with more than all the fires of her own. In the excitement of my opium dreams (for I was habitually fettered in the shackles of the drug), I would call aloud upon her name, during the silence of the night, or among the sheltered recesses of the glens by day, as if, through the wild eagerness, the solemn passion, the consuming ardor of my longing for the departed, I could restore her to the pathways she had abandoned — ah, *could* it be forever? — upon the earth.

About the commencement of the second month of the marriage, the Lady Rowena was attacked with sudden illness, from which her recovery was slow. The fever which consumed her rendered her nights uneasy; and in her perturbed state of half-slumber, she

spoke of sounds, and of motions, in and about
the chamber of the turret, which I concluded
had no origin save in the distemper of her
fancy, or perhaps in the phantasmagoric influences of the chamber itself. She became
at length convalescent — finally, well. Yet
but a brief period elapsed, ere a second more
violent disorder again threw her upon a bed
of suffering; and from this attack her frame,
at all times feeble, never altogether recovered. Her illnesses were, after this epoch, of
alarming character, and more alarming re-
currence, defying alike the knowledge and
the great exertions of her physicians. With
the increase of the chronic disease, which
had thus, apparently, taken too sure hold
upon her constitution to be eradicated by
human means, I could not fail to observe a
similar increase in the nervous irritation of
her temperament, and in her excitability by
trivial causes of fear. She spoke again, and
now more frequently and pertinaciously, of
the sounds — of the slight sounds — and of
the unusual motions among the tapestries,
to which she had formerly alluded.

One night, near the closing in of September, she pressed this distressing subject with

more than usual emphasis upon my attention.
She had just awakened from an unquiet
slumber, and I had been watching, with feelings half of anxiety, half of vague terror, the
workings of her emaciated countenance. I sat
by the side of her ebony bed, upon one of the
ottomans of India. She partly arose, and
spoke, in an earnest low whisper, of sounds
which she *then* heard, but which I could not
hear — of motions which she *then* saw, but
which I could not perceive. The wind was
rushing hurriedly behind the tapestries, and
I wished to show her (what, let me confess
it, I could not *all* believe) that those almost
inarticulate breathings, and those very gentle
variations of the figures upon the wall, were
but the natural effects of that customary
rushing of the wind. But a deadly pallor,
overspreading her face, had proved to me
that my exertions to reassure her would be
fruitless. She appeared to be fainting, and
no attendants were within call. I remembered
where was deposited a decanter of light wine
which had been ordered by her physicians,
and hastened across the chamber to procure
it. But, as I stepped beneath the light of the
censer, two circumstances of a startling na-

ture attracted my attention. I had felt that
some palpable although invisible object had
passed lightly by my person; and I saw that
there lay upon the golden carpet, in the very
middle of the rich luster thrown from the
censer, a shadow — a faint, indefinite shadow
of angelic aspect — such as might be fancied
for the shadow of a shade. But I was wild
with the excitement of an immoderate dose
of opium, and heeded these things but little,
nor spoke of them to Rowena. Having found
the wine, I recrossed the chamber, and poured
out a gobletful, which I held to the lips of
the fainting lady. She had now partially recovered, however, and took the vessel herself,
while I sank upon an ottoman near me, with
my eyes fastened upon her person. It was
then that I became distinctly aware of a gentle footfall upon the carpet, and near the
couch; and in a second thereafter, as Rowena
was in the act of raising the wine to her lips,
I saw, or may have dreamed that I saw, fall
within the goblet, as if from some invisible
spring in the atmosphere of the room, three
or four large drops of a brilliant and ruby-
colored fluid. If this I saw — not so Rowena.
She swallowed the wine unhesitatingly, and

I forbore to speak to her of a circumstance which must, after all, I considered, have been but the suggestion of a vivid imagination, rendered morbidly active by the terror of the lady, by the opium, and by the hour.

Yet I cannot conceal it from my own perception that, immediately subsequent to the fall of the ruby drops, a rapid change for the worse took place in the disorder of my wife; so that, on the third subsequent night, the hands of her menials prepared her for the tomb, and on the fourth, I sat alone, with her shrouded body, in that fantastic chamber which had received her as my bride. Wild visions, opium-engendered, flitted, shadow-like, before me. I gazed with unquiet eye upon the sarcophagi in the angles of the room, upon the varying figures of the drapery, and upon the writhing of the particolored fires in the censer overhead. My eyes then fell, as I called to mind the circumstances of a former night, to the spot beneath the glare of the censer where I had seen the faint traces of the shadow. It was there, however, no longer; and breathing with greater freedom, I turned my glances to the pallid and rigid figure upon the bed. Then rushed upon me a thousand

memories of Ligeia — and then came back
upon my heart, with the turbulent violence of
a flood, the whole of that unutterable woe
with which I had regarded *her* thus enshrouded. The night waned and still, with a
bosom full of bitter thoughts of the one and
only and supremely beloved, I remained gazing upon the body of Rowena.

It might have been midnight, or perhaps
earlier or later, for I had taken no note of
time, when a sob, low, gentle, but very distinct, startled me from my revery. I *felt* that
it came from the bed of ebony — the bed of
death. I listened in an agony of superstitious
terror — but there was no repetition of the
sound. I strained my vision to detect any
motion in the corpse — but there was not the
slightest perceptible. Yet I could not have
been deceived. I *had* heard the noise, however
faint, and my soul was awakened within me.
I resolutely and perseveringly kept my attention riveted upon the body. Many minutes
elapsed before any circumstance occurred
tending to throw light upon the mystery. At
length it became evident that a slight, a very
feeble, and barely noticeable tinge of color
had flushed up within the cheeks, and along

the sunken small veins of eyelids. Through a
species of unutterable horror and awe, for
which the language of mortality has no
sufficiently energetic expression, I felt my
heart cease to beat, my limbs grow rigid
where I sat. Yet a sense of duty finally operated to restore my self-possession. I could no
longer doubt that we had been precipitate in
our preparations — that Rowena still lived. It
was necessary that some immediate exertion
be made; yet the turret was altogether apart
from the portion of the abbey tenanted by the
servants — there were none within call — I
had no means of summoning them to my aid
without leaving the room for many minutes
— and this I could not venture to do. I therefore struggled alone in my endeavors to call
back the spirit still hovering. In a short
period it was certain, however, that a relapse
had taken place; the color disappeared from
both eyelid and cheek, leaving a wanness even
more than that of marble; the lips became
doubly shriveled and pinched up in the
ghastly expression of death; a repulsive clam-
miness and coldness overspread rapidly the
surface of the body; and all the usual rigorous
stiffness immediately supervened. I fell back

with a shudder upon the couch from which I
had been so startlingly aroused, and again
gave myself up to passionate waking visions
of Ligeia.

An hour thus elapsed, when (could it be
possible?) I was a second time aware of some
vague sound issuing from the region of the
bed. I listened — in extremity of horror. The
sound came again — it was a sigh. Rushing to
the corpse, I saw — distinctly saw — a
tremor upon the lips. In a minute afterward
they relaxed, disclosing a bright line of the
pearly teeth. Amazement now struggled in
my bosom with the profound awe which had
hitherto reigned there alone. I felt that my
vision grew dim, that my reason wandered;
and it was only by a violent effort that I at
length succeeded in nerving myself to the task
which duty thus once more had pointed out.
There was now a partial glow upon the forehead and upon the cheek and throat; a perceptible warmth pervaded the whole frame;
there was even a slight pulsation at the heart.
The lady *lived;* and with redoubled ardor I
betook myself to the task of restoration. I
chafed and bathed the temples and the hands,
and used every exertion which experience,

and no little medical reading, could suggest.
But in vain. Suddenly, the color fled, the pulsation ceased, the lips resumed the expression
of the dead, and, in an instant afterward, the
whole body took upon itself the icy chilliness,
the livid hue, the intense rigidity, the sunken
outline, and all the loathsome peculiarities of
that which has been, for many days, a tenant
of the tomb.

And again I sunk into visions of Ligeia —
and again (what marvel that I shudder while
I write?), *again* there reached my ears a low
sob from the region of the ebony bed. But
why shall I minutely detail the unspeakable
horrors of that night? Why shall I pause to
relate how, time after time, until near the
period of the gray dawn, this hideous drama
of revivification was repeated; how each terrific relapse was only into a sterner and apparently more irredeemable death; how each
agony wore the aspect of a struggle with some
invisible foe; and how each struggle was succeeded by I know not what of wild change in
the personal appearance of the corpse? Let
me hurry to a conclusion.

The greater part of the fearful night had
worn away, and she who had been dead once

again stirred — and now more vigorously
than hitherto, although arousing from a dissolution more appalling in its utter hopelessness than any. I had long ceased to struggle
or to move, and remained sitting rigidly upon
the ottoman, a helpless prey to a whirl of violent emotions, of which extreme awe was perhaps the least terrible, the least consuming.
The corpse, I repeat, stirred, and now more
vigorously than before. The hues of life
flushed up with unwonted energy into the
countenance — the limbs relaxed — and, save
that the eyelids were yet pressed heavily together, and that the bandages and draperies
of the grave still imparted their charnel
character to the figure, I might have dreamed
that Rowena had indeed shaken off, utterly,
the fetters of Death. But if this idea was not,
even then, altogether adopted, I could at least
doubt no longer, when, arising from the bed,
tottering, with feeble steps, with closed eyes,
and with the manner of one bewildered in a
dream, the thing that was enshrouded advanced boldly and palpably into the middle of
the apartment.

I trembled not — I stirred not — for a
crowd of unutterable fancies connected with

the air, the stature, the demeanor, of the figure, rushing hurriedly through my brain, had paralyzed — had chilled me into stone. I stirred not — but gazed upon the apparition. There was a mad disorder in my thoughts — a tumult unappeasable. Could it, indeed, be the *living* Rowena who confronted me? Could it, indeed, be Rowena *at all* — the fair-haired, the blue-eyed Lady Rowena Trevanion of Tremaine? Why, *why* should I doubt it? The bandage lay heavily about the mouth — but then might it not be the mouth of the breathing Lady of Tremaine? And the cheeks — there were the roses as in her noon of life — yes, these might indeed be the fair cheeks of the living Lady of Tremaine. And the chin, with its dimples, as in health, might it not be hers? — but *had she then grown taller since her* malady? What inexpressible madness seized me with that thought? One bound, and I had reached her feet! Shrinking from my touch, she let fall from her head, unloosened, the ghastly cerements which had confined it, and there streamed forth into the rushing atmosphere of the chamber huge masses of long and disheveled hair; *it was blacker than the raven wings of midnight!* And now slowly

opened *the eyes* of the figure which stood
before me. "Here then, at least," I shrieked
aloud, "can I never — can I never be mis-
taken — these are the full, and the black, and
the wild eyes — of my lost love — of the
Lady — of the LADY LIGEIA."

The Fall
of the
House of Usher

First published in *Burton's Gentleman's Magazine* for September, 1839, this story is perhaps Poe's best effort to achieve "unity of effect or impression," a phrase which appears in his own review of Hawthorne's *Twice-Told Tales*. What is this "effect" or "impression"? We may choose from a list of Poe's atmosphere words: gloom, melancholy, decay, dreariness, dilapidation, etc. Or we may see Roderick Usher as the key to Poe's "unique or single effect," and select from words like "instability," "terror," "hysteria." For Roderick, the house is full of sinister pulsations: the very stones, he senses, are decomposing like vegetable matter; and between Roderick and his twin sister there are invisible wires, "sympathies of a scarcely intelligible nature." Even after her premature burial, the wires continue to hum — until it is *time* for the ghastly reunion. Then, and only then, can the doomed house crumble into the black pond.

Son cœur est un luth suspendu;
Sitôt qu'on le touche il résonne.
— *De Béranger*

During the whole of a dull, dark, and soundless day in the autumn of the year, when the clouds hung oppressively low in the heavens, I had been passing alone, on horseback, through a singularly dreary tract of country, and at length found myself, as the shades of the evening drew on, within view of the melancholy House of Usher. I know not how it was — but, with the first glimpse of the building, a sense of insufferable gloom pervaded my spirit. I say insufferable; for the feeling was unrelieved by any of that half-pleasurable, because poetic, sentiment with which the mind usually receives even the sternest natural images of the desolate or terrible. I looked upon the scene before me— upon the mere house, and the simple landscape features of the domain — upon the bleak walls — upon the vacant eyelike windows — upon a few rank sedges — and upon a few white trunks of decayed trees — with an utter depression of soul which I can compare to no earthly sensation more properly than to the afterdream of the reveler upon opium — the bitter lapse into everyday life — the hideous dropping off of the veil. There was an iciness, a sinking, a sickening of the heart — an unredeemed dreariness of thought which no goading of the imagination could torture into aught of the sublime. What was it — I paused to think — what was it that so unnerved me in the contemplation of the House of Usher? It was a mystery all insoluble; nor could I grapple with the shadowy fancies that crowded upon me as I pondered. I was forced to fall back upon the unsatisfactory conclusion that while, beyond doubt, there *are* combinations of very simple natural objects which have the power of thus affecting us,

still the analysis of this power lies among
considerations beyond our depth. It was possible, I reflected, that a mere different
arrangement of the particulars of the scene,
of the details of the picture, would be sufficient to modify, or perhaps to annihilate, its
capacity for sorrowful impression; and, acting upon this idea, I reined my horse to the
precipitous brink of a black and lurid tarn
that lay in unruffled luster by the dwelling,
and gazed down — but with a shudder even
more thrilling than before — upon the re-
modeled and inverted images of the gray
sedge, and the ghastly tree stems, and the
vacant and eye-like windows.

Nevertheless, in this mansion of gloom I
now proposed to myself a sojourn of some
weeks. Its proprietor, Roderick Usher, had
been one of my boon companions in boyhood;
but many years had elapsed since our last
meeting. A letter, however, had lately reached
me in a distant part of the country — a letter
from him — which, in its wildly importunate
nature, had admitted of no other than a
personal reply. The MS. gave evidence of
nervous agitation. The writer spoke of acute
bodily illness — of a mental disorder which

oppressed him — and of an earnest desire to see me, as his best and indeed his only personal friend, with a view of attempting, by the cheerfulness of my society, some alleviation of his malady. It was the manner in which all this, and much more, was said — it was the apparent *heart* that went with his request — which allowed me no room for hesitation; and I accordingly obeyed forthwith what I still considered a very singular summons.

Although, as boys, we had been even intimate associates, yet I really knew little of my friend. His reserve had been always excessive and habitual. I was aware, however, that his very ancient family had been noted, time out of mind, for a peculiar sensibility of temperament, displaying itself, through long ages, in many works of exalted art, and manifested, of late, in repeated deeds of munificent yet unobtrusive charity, as well as in a passionate devotion to the intricacies, perhaps even more than to the orthodox and easily recognizable beauties, of musical science. I had learned, too, the very remarkable fact, that the stem of the Usher race, all time-honored as it was, had put forth, at no period, any enduring branch; in other words, that the entire family lay in the direct line of descent, and had always, with very trifling and very temporary variation, so lain. It was this deficiency, I considered, while running over in thought the perfect keeping of the character of the premises with the accredited character of the people, and while speculating upon the possible influence which the one, in the long lapse of centuries, might have exercised upon the other — it was this deficiency, perhaps, of collateral issue, and the consequent undeviating transmission, from sire to son, of the patrimony with the name, which had, at length, so identified the two as to merge the original title of the estate in the quaint and equivocal appellation of the "House of Usher" — an appellation which seemed to include, in the minds of the peasantry who used it, both the family and the family mansion.

I have said that the sole effect of my somewhat childish experiment — that of looking down within the tarn — had been to deepen the first singular impression. There can be no doubt that the consciousness of the rapid increase of my superstition — for why should I not so term it? — served mainly to accelerate the increase itself. Such, I have long known, is the paradoxical law of all sentiments having terror as a basis. And it might have been for this reason only, that, when I again uplifted my eyes to the house itself, from its image in the pool, there grew in my mind a strange fancy — a fancy so ridiculous, indeed, that I but mention it to show the vivid force of the sensations which oppressed me. I had so worked upon my imagination as really to believe that about the whole mansion and domain there hung an atmosphere peculiar to themselves and their immediate vicinity — an atmosphere which had no affinity with the air of heaven, but which had reeked up from the decayed trees, and the gray wall, and the silent tarn — a pestilent and mystic vapor, dull, sluggish, faintly discernible, and leaden-hued.

Shaking off from my spirit what *must* have been a dream, I scanned more narrowly the real aspect of the building. Its principal feature seemed to be that of an excessive antiquity. The discoloration of ages had been great. Minute fungi overspread the whole exterior, hanging in a fine tangled webwork from the eaves. Yet all this was apart from any extraordinary dilapidation. No portion of the masonry had fallen, and there appeared to be a wild inconsistency between its still perfect adaptation of parts and the crumbling condition of the individual stones. In this there was much that reminded me of the specious totality of old woodwork which has rotted for long years in some neglected vault, with no disturbance from the breath of the external air. Beyond this indication of extensive decay, however, the fabric gave little token of instability. Perhaps the eye of a scrutinizing observer might have discovered a barely perceptible fissure, which, extending from the roof of the building in front, made its way down the wall in a zigzag direction, until it became lost in the sullen waters of the tarn.

Noticing these things, I rode over a short causeway to the house. A servant in waiting took my horse, and I entered the Gothic archway of the hall. A valet, of stealthy step, thence conducted me, in silence, through many dark and intricate passages in my progress to the studio of his master. Much that I encountered on the way contributed, I know not how, to heighten the vague senti-

ments of which I have already spoken. While
the objects around me — while the carvings
of the ceilings, the somber tapestries of the
walls, the ebon blackness of the floors, and
the phantasmagoric armorial trophies which
rattled as I strode, were but matters to which,
or to such as which, I had been accustomed
from my infancy — while I hesitated not to
acknowledge how familiar was all this — I
still wondered to find how unfamiliar were
the fancies which ordinary images were
stirring up. On one of the staircases, I met
the physician of the family. His countenance,
I thought, wore a mingled expression of low
cunning and perplexity. He accosted me with
trepidation and passed on. The valet now
threw open a door and ushered me into the
presence of his master.

The room in which I found myself was very
large and lofty. The windows were long,
narrow, and pointed, and at so vast a distance
from the black oaken floor as to be altogether
inaccessible from within. Feeble gleams of
encrimsoned light made their way through
the trellised panes, and served to render
sufficiently distinct the more prominent
objects around; the eye, however, struggled

in vain to reach the remoter angles of the
chamber, or the recesses of the vaulted and
fretted ceiling. Dark draperies hung upon the
walls. The general furniture was profuse,
comfortless, antique, and tattered. Many
books and musical instruments lay scattered
about, but failed to give any vitality to the
scene. I felt that I breathed an atmosphere
of sorrow. An air of stern, deep, and irredeemable gloom hung over and pervaded all.

Upon my entrance, Usher arose from a sofa
on which he had been lying at full length, and
greeted me with a vivacious warmth which
had much in it, I at first thought, of an over-
done cordiality — of the constrained effort of
the *ennuyé* man of the world. A glance, however, at his countenance convinced me of his
perfect sincerity. We sat down; and for some
moments, while he spoke not, I gazed upon
him with a feeling half of pity, half of awe.
Surely, man had never before so terribly
altered, in so brief a period, as had Roderick
Usher! It was with difficulty that I could bring
myself to admit the identity of the wan being
before me with the companion of my early
boyhood. Yet the character of his face had
been at all times remarkable. A cadaverous-

ness of complexion; an eye large, liquid, and luminous beyond comparison; lips somewhat thin and very pallid, but of a surpassingly beautiful curve; a nose of a delicate Hebrew model, but with a breadth of nostril unusual in similar formations; a finely molded chin, speaking, in its want of prominence, of a want of moral energy; hair of a more than weblike softness and tenuity — these features, with an inordinate expansion above the regions of the temple, made up altogether a countenance not easily to be forgotten. And now in the mere exaggeration of the prevailing character of these features, and of the expression they were wont to convey, lay so much of change that I doubted to whom I spoke. The now ghastly pallor of the skin, and the now miraculous luster of the eye, above all things startled and even awed me. The silken hair, too, had been suffered to grow all unheeded, and as, in its wild gossamer texture, it floated rather than fell about the face, I could not, even with effort, connect its arabesque expression with any idea of simple humanity.

In the manner of my friend I was at once struck with an incoherence — an inconsistency; and I soon found this to arise from a series of feeble and futile struggles to overcome an habitual trepidancy — an excessive nervous agitation. For something of this nature I had indeed been prepared, no less by his letter than by reminiscences of certain boyish traits, and by conclusions deduced from his peculiar physical confirmation and temperament. His action was alternately vivacious and sullen. His voice varied rapidly from a tremulous indecision (when the animal spirits seemed utterly in abeyance) to that species of energetic concision — that abrupt, weighty, unhurried, and hollow-sounding enunciation — that leaden, self-balanced, and perfectly modulated guttural utterance, which may be observed in the lost drunkard, or the irreclaimable eater of opium, during the periods of his most intense excitement.

It was thus that he spoke of the object of my visit, of his earnest desire to see me, and of the solace he expected me to afford him. He entered, at some length, into what he conceived to be the nature of his malady. It was, he said, a constitutional and a family evil, and one for which he despaired to find a remedy

— a mere nervous affection, he immediately
added, which would undoubtedly soon pass
off. It displayed itself in a host of unnatural
sensations. Some of these, as he detailed
them, interested and bewildered me; although, perhaps, the terms and the general
manner of their narration had their weight.
He suffered much from a morbid acuteness
of the senses; the most insipid food was alone
endurable; he could wear only garments of
certain texture; the odors of all flowers were
oppressive; his eyes were tortured by even a
faint light; and there were but peculiar
sounds, and these from stringed instruments,
which did not inspire him with horror.

To an anomalous species of terror I found
him a bounden slave. "I shall perish," said he,
"*I must perish* in this deplorable folly. Thus,
thus and not otherwise, shall I be lost. I dread
the events of the future, not in themselves,
but in their results. I shudder at the thought
of any, even the most trivial, incident which
may operate upon this intolerable agitation of
soul. I have, indeed, no abhorrence of danger,
except in its absolute effect — in terror. In
this unnerved, in this pitiable, condition I
feel that the period will sooner or later arrive

when I must abandon life and reason together, in some struggle with the grim phantasm, FEAR."

I learned, moreover, at intervals, and through broken and equivocal hints, another singular feature of his mental condition. He was enchained by certain superstitious impressions in regard to the dwelling which he tenanted, and whence, for many years, he had never ventured forth — in regard to an influence whose superstitious force was conveyed in terms too shadowy here to be restated — an influence which some peculiarities in the mere form and substance of his family mansion had, by dint of long sufferance, he said, obtained over his spirit — an effect which the *physique* of the gray walls and turrets, and of the dim tarn into which they all looked down, had, at length, brought about upon the *morale* of his existence.

He admitted, however, although with hesitation, that much of the peculiar gloom which thus afflicted him could be traced to a more natural and far more palpable origin — to the severe and long-continued illness, indeed to the evidently approaching dissolution — of a tenderly beloved sister, his sole companion for long years, his last and only relative on earth. "Her decease," he said, with a bitterness which I can never forget, "would leave him (him, the hopeless and the frail) the last of the ancient race of the Ushers." While he spoke, the Lady Madeline (for so was she called) passed through a remote portion of the apartment, and, without having noticed my presence, disappeared. I regarded her with an utter astonishment not unmingled with dread; and yet I found it impossible to account for such feelings. A sensation of stupor oppressed me as my eyes followed her retreating steps. When a door, at length, closed upon her, my glance sought instinctively and eagerly the countenance of the brother; but he had buried his face in his hands, and I could only perceive that a far more than ordinary wanness had overspread the emaciated fingers through which trickled many passionate tears.

The disease of the Lady Madeline had long baffled the skill of her physicians. A settled apathy, a gradual wasting away of the person, and frequent although transient affections of a partially cataleptical character were the unusual diagnosis. Hitherto she had steadily borne up against the pressure of her malady, and had not betaken herself finally to bed; but on the closing in of the evening of my arrival at the house, she succumbed (as her brother told me at night with inexpressible agitation) to the prostrating power of the destroyer; and I learned that the glimpse I had obtained of her person would thus probably be the last I should obtain — that the lady, at least while living, would be seen by me no more.

For several days ensuing, her name was unmentioned by either Usher or myself; and during this period I was busied in earnest endeavors to alleviate the melancholy of my friend. We painted and read together, or I listened, as if in a dream, to the wild improvisations of his speaking guitar. And thus, as a closer and still closer intimacy admitted me more unreservedly into the recesses of his spirit, the more bitterly did I perceive the futility of all attempt at cheering a mind from which darkness, as if an inherent positive quality, poured forth upon all objects of the moral and physical universe in one unceasing radiation of gloom.

I shall ever bear about me a memory of the

many solemn hours I thus spent alone with
the master of the House of Usher. Yet I
should fail in any attempt to convey an idea
of the exact character of the studies, or of the
occupations, in which he involved me, or led
me the way. An excited and highly dis-
tempered ideality threw a sulfureous luster
over all. His long improvised dirges will ring
forever in my ears. Among other things, I
hold painfully in mind a certain singular per-
version and amplification of the wild air of
the last waltz of Von Weber. From the paintings over which his elaborate fancy brooded,
and which grew, touch by touch, into vague-
nesses at which I shuddered the more thrillingly, because I shuddered knowing not why
— from these paintings (vivid as their
images now are before me) I would in vain
endeavor to educe more than a small portion
which should lie within the compass of
merely written words. By the utter simplic-
ity, by the nakedness of his designs, he
arrested and overawed attention. If ever
mortal painted an idea, that mortal was
Roderick Usher. For me at least, in the circumstances then surrounding me, there arose
out of the pure abstractions which the hypo-

chondriac contrived to throw upon his canvas, an intensity of intolerable awe, no shadow of which felt I ever yet in the contemplation of the certainly glowing yet too concrete reveries of Fuseli.

One of the phantasmagoric conceptions of my friend, partaking not so rigidly of the spirit of abstraction, may be shadowed forth, although feebly, in words. A small picture presented the interior of an immensely long and rectangular vault or tunnel, with low walls, smooth, white, and without interruption or device. Certain accessory points of the design served well to convey the idea that this excavation lay at an exceeding depth below the surface of the earth. No outlet was observed in any portion of its vast extent, and no torch or other artificial source of light was discernible; yet a flood of intense rays rolled throughout, and bathed the whole in a ghastly and inappropriate splendor.

I have just spoken of the morbid condition of the auditory nerve which rendered all music intolerable to the sufferer, with the exception of certain effects of stringed instruments. It was, perhaps, the narrow limits to which he thus confined himself upon the

guitar which gave birth, in great measure,
to the fantastic character of his perform-
ances. But the fervid facility of his impromp-
tus could not be so accounted for. They must
have been, and were, in the notes, as well as
in the words of his wild fantasias (for he not
unfrequently accompanied himself with
rhymed verbal improvisations), the result of
that intense mental collectedness and concen-
tration to which I have previously alluded as
observable only in particular moments of the
highest artificial excitement. The words of
one of these rhapsodies I have easily remembered. I was, perhaps, the more forcibly impressed with it as he gave it, because, in the
under or mystic current of its meaning, I
fancied that I perceived, and for the first
time, a full consciousness on the part of
Usher of the tottering of his lofty reason
upon her throne. The verses, which were entitled "The Haunted Palace," ran very nearly,
if not accurately, thus:

In the greenest of our valleys,
    By good angels tenanted,
Once a fair and stately palace —
    Radiant palace — reared its head.

In the monarch Thought's dominion —
   It stood there!
Never seraph spread a pinion
   Over fabric half so fair.

Banners yellow, glorious, golden,
   On its roof did float and flow;
(This — all this — was in the olden
   Time long ago)
And every gentle air that dallied,
   In that sweet day,
Along the ramparts plumed and pallid,
   A winged odor went away.

Wanderers in that happy valley
   Through two luminous windows saw
Spirits moving musically
   To a lute's well-tuned law,
Round about a throne, where sitting
   (Porphyrogene!)
In state his glory well befitting,
   The ruler of the realm was seen.

And all with pearl and ruby glowing
   Was the fair palace door,
Through which came flowing, flowing, flowing
   And sparkling evermore,
A troop of Echoes whose sweet duty
   Was but to sing,
In voices of surpassing beauty,
   The wit and wisdom of their king.

But evil things, in robes of sorrow,
   Assailed the monarch's high estate;
(Ah, let us mourn, for never morrow
   Shall dawn upon him, desolate!)
And, round about his home, the glory
   That blushed and bloomed
Is but a dim-remembered story
   Of the old time entombed.

And travelers now within that valley,
   Through the red-litten windows, see
Vast forms that move fantastically
   To a discordant melody;
While, like a rapid ghastly river,
   Through the pale door,
A hideous throng rush out forever,
   And laugh — but smile no more.

I well remember that suggestions arising
from this ballad led us into a train of thought
wherein there became manifest an opinion of
Usher's which I mention not so much on
account of its novelty (for other men have
thought thus), as on account of the pertinac-
ity with which he maintained it. This opinion,
in its general form, was that of the sentience
of all vegetable things. But, in his disordered
fancy, the idea had assumed a more daring
character, and trespassed, under certain con-

ditions, upon the kingdom of inorganization. I lack words to express the full extent, or the earnest *abandon* of his persuasion. The belief, however, was connected (as I have previously hinted) with the gray stones of the home of his forefathers. The conditions of the sentience had been here, he imagined, fulfilled in the method of collocation of these stones — in the order of their arrangement, as well as in that of the many fungi which overspread them, and of the decayed trees which stood around — above all, in the long undisturbed endurance of this arrangement, and in its reduplication in the still waters of the tarn. Its evidence — the evidence of the sentience — was to be seen, he said, (and I here started as he spoke,) in the gradual yet certain condensation of an atmosphere of their own about the waters and the walls. The result was discoverable, he added, in that silent, yet importunate and terrible influence which for centuries had molded the destinies of his family, and which made *him* what I now saw him — what he was. Such opinions need no comment, and I will make none.

Our books — the books which, for years, had formed no small portion of the mental

existence of the invalid — were, as might be
supposed, in strict keeping with this character of phantasm. We pored together over
such works as the *Ververt et Chartreuse* of
Gresset; the *Belphegor* of Machiavelli; the
Heaven and Hell of Swedenborg; the *Sub-
terranean Voyage of Nicholas Klimm* of Hol-
berg; the *Chiromancy* of Robert Flud, of Jean
d'Indaginé, and of De la Chambre; the
Journey into the Blue Distance of Tieck; and
the *City of the Sun* of Campanella. One
favorite volume was a small octavo edition of
the *Directorium Inquisitorium*, by the
Dominican Eymeric de Gironne; and there
were passages in Pomponius Mela, about the
old African Satyrs and Egipans, over which
Usher would sit dreaming for hours. His
chief delight, however, was found in the
perusal of an exceedingly rare and curious
book in quarto Gothic—the manual of a forgotten church — *the Vigiliæ Mortuorum
secundum Chorum Ecclesiæ Maguntinæ.*

I could not help thinking of the wild ritual
of this work, and of its probable influence
upon the hypochondriac, when, one evening,
having informed me abruptly that the Lady
Madeline was no more, he stated his intention

of preserving her corpse for a forthnight
(previously to its final interment), in one of
the numerous vaults within the main walls of
the building. The worldly reason, however,
assigned for this singular proceeding, was
one which I did not feel at liberty to dispute.
The brother had been led to his resolution (so
he told me) by consideration of the unusual
character of the malady of the deceased, of
certain obtrusive and eager inquiries on the
part of her medical men, and of the remote
and exposed situation of the burial ground
of the family. I will not deny that when I
called to mind the sinister countenance of the
person whom I met upon the staircase, on the
day of my arrival at the house, I had no desire
to oppose what I regarded as at best but a
harmless, and by no means an unnatural,
precaution.

At the request of Usher, I personally aided
him in the arrangements for the temporary
entombment. The body having been en-
coffined, we two alone bore it to its rest. The
vault in which we placed it (and which had
been so long unopened that our torches, half
smothered in its oppressive atmosphere, gave
us little opportunity for investigation) was

small, damp, and entirely without means of admission for light; lying, at great depth, immediately beneath that portion of the building in which was my own sleeping apartment. It had been used, apparently, in remote feudal times, for the worst purposes of a donjon keep, and, in later days, as a place of deposit for powder, or some other highly combustible substance, as a portion of its floor, and the whole interior of a long archway through which we reached it, were carefully sheathed with copper. The door, of massive iron, had been, also, similarly protected. Its immense weight caused an unusually sharp, grating sound, as it moved upon its hinges.

Having deposited our mournful burden upon tressels within this region of horror, we partially turned aside the yet unscrewed lid of the coffin, and looked upon the face of the tenant. A striking similitude between the brother and sister now first arrested my attention; and Usher, divining, perhaps, my thoughts, murmured out some few words from which I learned that the deceased and himself had been twins, and that sympathies of a scarcely intelligible nature had always existed between them. Our glances, however, rested not long upon the dead — for we could not regard her unawed. The disease which had thus entombed the lady in the maturity of youth, had left, as usual in all maladies of a strictly cataleptical character, the mockery of a faint blush upon the bosom and the face, and that suspiciously lingering smile upon the lip which is so terrible in death. We replaced and screwed down the lid, and, having secured the door of iron, made our way, with toil, into the scarcely less gloomy apartments of the upper portion of the house.

And now, some days of bitter grief having elapsed, an observable change came over the features of the mental disorder of my friend. His ordinary manner had vanished. His ordinary occupations were neglected or forgotten. He roamed from chamber to chamber with hurried, unequal, and objectless step. The pallor of his countenance had assumed, if possible, a more ghastly hue — but the luminousness of his eye had utterly gone out. The once occasional huskiness of his tone was heard no more; and a tremulous quaver, as if of extreme terror, habitually characterized his utterance. There were times, indeed, when I thought his unceasingly agitated mind was laboring with some oppressive secret, to divulge which he struggled for the necessary courage. At times, again, I was obliged to resolve all into the mere inexplicable vagaries of madness, for I beheld him gazing upon vacancy for long hours, in an attitude of the profoundest attention, as if listening to some imaginary sound. It was no wonder that his condition terrified — that it infected me. I felt creeping upon me, by slow yet certain degrees, the wild influences of his own fantastic yet impressive superstitions.

It was, especially, upon retiring to bed late in the night of the seventh or eighth day after the placing of the Lady Madeline within the donjon, that I experienced the full power of such feelings. Sleep came not near my couch — while the hours waned and waned away. I struggled to reason off the nervousness which had dominion over me. I endeavored to believe that much, if not all of what I felt, was due to the bewildering influence of the gloomy furniture of the room — of the dark and tattered draperies, which, tortured into motion by the breath of a rising tempest, swayed fitfully to and fro upon the walls, and rustled uneasily about the decorations of the bed. But my efforts were fruitless. An irrepressible tremor gradually pervaded my frame; and, at length, there sat upon my very heart an incubus of utterly causeless alarm. Shaking this off with a gasp and a struggle, I uplifted myself upon the pillows, and, peering earnestly within the intense darkness of the chamber, hearkened — I know not why, except that an instinctive spirit prompted me — to certain low and indefinite sounds which came, through the pauses of the storm, at long intervals, I know not whence. Overpowered by an intense sentiment of horror, unaccountable yet unendurable, I threw on my clothes with haste (for I felt that I should sleep no more during the night), and endeavored to arouse myself from the pitiable condition into which I had fallen, by pacing rapidly to and fro through the apartment.

I had taken but few turns in this manner when a light step on an adjoining staircase arrested my attention. I presently recognized it as that of Usher. In an instant afterward he rapped, with a gentle touch, at my door, and entered, bearing a lamp. His countenance was, as usual, cadaverously wan — but, moreover, there was a species of mad hilarity in his eyes — an evidently restrained hysteria in his whole demeanor. His air appalled me — but anything was preferable to the solitude which I had so long endured, and I even welcomed his presence as a relief.

"And you have not seen it?" he said abruptly, after having stared about him for some moments in silence. "You have not then seen it? — but, stay! you shall." Thus speaking, and having carefully shaded his lamp, he hurried to one of the casements, and threw it freely open to the storm.

The impetuous fury of the entering gust nearly lifted us from our feet. It was, indeed, a tempestuous yet sternly beautiful night, and one wildly singular in its terror and its beauty. A whirlwind had apparently collected its force in our vicinity for there were frequent and violent alterations in the direction of the wind; and the exceeding density of the clouds (which hung so low as to press upon the turrets of the house) did not prevent our perceiving the lifelike velocity with which they flew careering from all points against each other, without passing away into the distance. I say that even their exceeding density did not prevent our perceiving this — yet we had no glimpse of the moon or stars, nor was there any flashing forth of the lightning. But the undersurfaces of the huge masses of agitated vapor, as well as all terrestrial objects immediately around us, were glowing in the unnatural light of a faintly luminous and distinctly visible gaseous exhalation which hung about and enshrouded the mansion.

"You must not — you shall not behold this!" said I, shuddering, to Usher, as I led him, with a gentle violence, from the window to a seat. "These appearances, which bewilder you, are merely electrical phenomena not uncommon — or it may be that they have their ghastly origin in the rank miasma of the tarn. Let us close this casement; the air is chilling and dangerous to your frame. Here is one of your favorite romances. I will read, and you shall listen — and so we will pass away this terrible night together."

The antique volume which I had taken up was the *Mad Trist* of Sir Launcelot Canning; but I had called it a favorite of Usher's more in sad jest than in earnest; for, in truth, there is little in its uncouth and unimaginative prolixity which could have had interest for the lofty and spiritual ideality of my friend. It was, however, the only book immediately at hand; and I indulged a vague hope that the excitement which now agitated the hypochondriac might find relief (for the history of mental disorder is full of similar anomalies) even in the extremeness of the folly which I should read. Could I have judged, indeed, by the wild overstrained air of vivacity with which he hearkened, or apparently hearkened, to the words of the tale, I might well have congratulated myself upon the success of my design.

I had arrived at that well-known portion of the story where Ethelred, the hero of the *Trist*, having sought in vain for peaceable admission into the dwelling of the hermit, proceeds to make good an entrance by force. Here, it will be remembered, the words of the narrative run thus:

"And Ethelred, who was by nature of a doughty heart, and who was now mighty withal, on account of the powerfulness of the wine which he had drunken, waited no longer to hold parley with the hermit, who, in sooth, was of an obstinate and maliceful turn, but, feeling the rain upon his shoulders, and fear-ing the rising of the tempest, uplifted his mace outright, and, with blows, made quickly room in the plankings of the door for his gauntleted hand; and now pulling therewith sturdily, he so cracked, and ripped, and tore all asunder, that the noise of the dry and hollow-sounding wood alarumed and reverberated throughout the forest."

At the termination of this sentence I started and, for a moment, paused; for it appeared to me (although I at once concluded that my excited fancy had deceived me) — it appeared to me that, from some very remote portion of the mansion, there came, indistinctly to my ears, what might have been, in its exact similarity of character, the echo (but a stifled and dull one certainly) of the very cracking and ripping sound which Sir Launcelot had so particularly described. It was, beyond doubt, the coincidence alone which had arrested my attention; for, amid the rattling of the sashes of the casements, and the ordinary commingled noises of the still increasing storm, the sound in itself had nothing, surely, which should have interested or disturbed me. I continued the story:

"But the good champion Ethelred, now

entering within the door, was sore enraged
and amazed to perceive no signal of the
maliceful hermit; but, in the stead thereof, a
dragon of a scaly and prodigious demeanor,
and of a fiery tongue, which sate in guard
before a palace of gold, with a floor of silver;
and upon the wall there hung a shield of
shining brass with this legend enwritten:

Who entereth herein, a conqueror hath bin;
Who slayeth the dragon, the shield he shall
win.

And Ethelred uplifted his mace, and struck
upon the head of the dragon, which fell before him, and gave up his pasty breath, with
a shriek so horrid and harsh, and withal so
piercing, that Ethelred had fain to close his
ears with his hands against the dreadful
noise of it, the like whereof was never before
heard."

Here again I paused abruptly, and now
with a feeling of wild amazement — for there
could be no doubt whatever that, in this instance, I did actually hear (although from
what direction it proceeded I found it impossible to say) a low and apparently distant,

but harsh, protracted, and most unusual screaming or grating sound — the exact counterpart of what my fancy had already conjured up for the dragon's unnatural shriek as described by the romancer.

Oppressed, as I certainly was, upon the occurrence of this second and most extraordinary coincidence, by a thousand conflicting sensations, in which wonder and extreme terror were predominant, I still retained sufficient presence of mind to avoid exciting, by any observation, the sensitive nervousness of my companion. I was by no means certain that he had noticed the sounds in question; although, assuredly, a strange alteration had, during the last few minutes, taken place in his demeanor. From a position fronting my own, he had gradually brought round his chair, so as to sit with his face to the door of the chamber; and thus I could but partially perceive his features, although I saw that his lips trembled as if he were murmuring inaudibly. His head had dropped upon his breast — yet I knew that he was not asleep, from the wide and rigid opening of the eye as I caught a glance of it in profile. The motion of his body, too, was at variance with this idea — for he rocked from side to side with a gentle yet constant and uniform sway. Having rapidly taken notice of all this, I resumed the narrative of Sir Launcelot, which thus proceeded:

"And now, the champion, having escaped from the terrible fury of the dragon, bethinking himself of the brazen shield, and of the breaking up of the enchantment which was upon it, removed the carcass from out of the way before him, and approached valorously over the silver pavement of the castle to where the shield was upon the wall; which in sooth tarried not for his full coming, but fell down at his feet upon the silver floor, with a mighty great and terrible ringing sound."

No sooner had these syllables passed my lips, than — as if a shield of brass had indeed, at the moment, fallen heavily upon a floor of silver — I became aware of a distinct, hollow, metallic, and clangorous, yet apparently muffled, reverberation. Completely unnerved, I leaped to my feet; but the measured rocking movement of Usher was undisturbed. I rushed to the chair in which he sat. His eyes were bent fixedly before him, and throughout his whole countenance there reigned a stony rigidity. But, as I placed my hand upon his shoulder, there came a strong shudder over his whole person; a sickly smile quivered about his lips; and I saw that he spoke in a low, hurried, and gibbering murmur, as if unconscious of my presence. Bending closely over him, I at length drank in the hideous import of his words.

"Now hear it? — yes, I hear it, and *have* heard it. Long — long — long — many minutes, many hours, many days have I heard it — yet I dared not — oh, pity me, miserable wretch that I am! — I dared not — I *dared* not speak! *We have put her living in the tomb!* Said I not that my senses were acute? I *now* tell you that I heard her first feeble movements in the hollow coffin. I heard them — many, many days ago — yet I dared not — *I dared not speak!* And now — tonight — Ethelred — ha! ha! — the breaking of the hermit's door, and the death cry of the dragon, and the clangor of the shield — say, rather, the rending of her coffin, and the grating of the iron hinges of her prison, and her struggles within the coppered archway of the vault! Oh! whither shall I fly? Will she

not be here anon? Is she not hurrying to up-
braid me for my haste? Have I not heard her
footstep on the stair? Do I distinguish that
heavy and horrible beating of her heart?
Madman!" — here he sprang furiously to his
feet, and shrieked out his syllables, as if in
the effort he were giving up his soul — *"Madman! I tell you that she now stands without
the door!"*

As if in the superhuman energy of his
utterance there had been found the potency
of a spell, the huge antique panels to which
the speaker pointed threw slowly back, upon
the instant, their ponderous and ebony jaws.
It was the work of the rushing gust — but
then without those doors there *did* stand the
lofty and enshrouded figure of the Lady
Madeline of Usher. There was blood upon her
white robes, and the evidence of some bitter
struggle upon every portion of her emaciated
frame. For a moment she remained trembling
and reeling to and fro upon the threshold —
then, with a low moaning cry, fell heavily in-
ward upon the person of her brother, and in
her violent and now final death agonies, bore
him to the floor a corpse, and a victim to the
terrors he had anticipated.

From that chamber, and from that mansion, I fled aghast. The storm was still abroad in all its wrath as I found myself crossing the old causeway. Suddenly there shot along the path a wild light, and I turned to see whence a gleam so unusual could have issued; for the vast house and its shadows were alone behind me. The radiance was that of the full, setting, and blood-red moon, which now shone vividly through that once barely discernible fissure, of which I have before spoken as extending from the roof of the building, in a zigzag direction, to the base. While I gazed, this fissure rapidly widened — there came a fierce breath of the whirlwind — the entire orb of the satellite burst at once upon my sight — my brain reeled as I saw the mighty walls rushing asunder — there was a long tumultuous shouting sound like the voice of a thousand waters — and the deep and dank tarn at my feet closed sullenly and silently over the fragments of the *"House of Usher."*

William Wilson

This story appeared in *Burton's Gentleman's* Magazine for October, 1839. William Wilson, a precocious child whose parents could do nothing to control, is sent to a school which could have been the very place that Poe attended at Stoke Newington, outside London. Wilson's natural superiority is accepted by most of his fellow students; but there is one boy, another William Wilson, who treats him as an equal. Wilson suffers much at the other's hands, and is happy to leave his tormentor behind when he enrolls at Eton, one of England's famous preparatory schools. But he has not escaped his namesake completely; like a patient detective, his double pursues him — seldom visible, but always at hand.

Is there a *lesson*? Possibly. Committed to being one person, Wilson discovers that his rampaging, aggressive self must come to terms with his conscience. Two William Wilsons cannot live in the same world. The outcome of their final encounter confirms our suspicions.

What say of it? what say conscience grim,
That spectre in my path?
                    — *Chamberlain*

Let me call myself, for the present,
William Wilson. The fair page now lying
before me need not be sullied with my real
appellation. This has been already too much
an object for the scorn — for the horror —
for the detestation of my race. To the utter-
most regions of the globe have not the indig-
nant winds bruited its unparalleled infamy?
Oh, outcast of all outcasts most abandoned!
— to the earth art thou not forever dead? to
its honors, to its flowers, to its golden aspirations? — and a cloud, dense, dismal, and

limitless, does it not hang eternally between thy hopes and heaven?

I would not, if I could, here or today, embody a record of my later years of unspeakable misery and unpardonable crime. This epoch — these later years — took unto themselves a sudden elevation in turpitude, whose origin alone it is my present purpose to assign. Men usually grow base by degrees. From me, in an instant, all virtue dropped bodily as a mantle. From comparatively trivial wickedness I passed, with the stride of a giant, into more than the enormities of an Elah-Gabalus. What chance — what one event brought this evil thing to pass, bear with me while I relate. Death approaches, and the shadow which foreruns him has thrown a softening influence over my spirit. I long, in passing through the dim valley, for the sympathy — I had nearly said for the pity — of my fellow men. I would fain have them believe that I have been, in some measure, the slave of circumstances beyond human control. I would wish them to seek out for me, in the details I am about to give, some little oasis of *fatality* amid a wilderness of error. I would have them allow — what they cannot refrain from allowing — that, although temptation may have erewhile existed as great, man was never *thus*, at least, tempted before — certainly, never *thus* fell. And is it therefore that he has never thus suffered? Have I not indeed been living in a dream? And am I not now dying a victim to the horror and the mystery of the wildest of all sublunary visions?

I am the descendant of a race whose imaginative and easily excitable temperament has at all times rendered them remarkable; and, in my earliest infancy, I gave evidence of having fully inherited the family character. As I advanced in years it was more strongly developed; becoming, for many reasons, a cause of serious disquietude to my friends, and of positive injury to myself. I grew self-willed, addicted to the wildest caprices, and a prey to the most ungovernable passions. Weakminded, and beset with constitutional infirmities akin to my own, my parents could do but little to check the evil propensities which distinguished me. Some feeble and ill-directed efforts resulted in complete failure on their part, and, of course, in total triumph on mine. Thenceforward my voice was a household law; and at an age when few children have abandoned their leading strings, I was left to the guidance of my own will, and became, in all but name, the master of my own actions.

My earliest recollections of a school life are connected with a large, rambling, Elizabethan house, in a misty-looking village of England, where were a vast number of gigantic and gnarled trees, and where all the houses were excessively ancient. In truth, it was a dreamlike and spirit-soothing place, that venerable old town. At this moment, in fancy, I feel the refreshing chilliness of its deeply shadowed avenues, inhale the fragrance of its thousand shrubberies, and thrill anew with undefinable delight at the deep hollow note of the church bell, breaking, each hour, with sullen and sudden roar, upon the stillness of the dusky atmosphere in which the fretted Gothic steeple lay imbedded and asleep.

It gives me, perhaps, as much of pleasure as I can now in any manner experience, to dwell upon minute recollections of the school and its concerns. Steeped in misery as I am — misery, alas! only too real — I shall be par-

doned for seeking relief, however slight and
temporary, in the weakness of a few rambling details. These, moreover, utterly trivial,
and even ridiculous in themselves, assume, to
my fancy, adventitious importance, as connected with a period and a locality when and
where I recognize the first ambiguous moni-
tions of the destiny which afterward so fully
overshadowed me. Let me then remember.

The house, I have said, was old and irregular. The grounds were extensive, and a high
and solid brick wall, topped with a bed of
mortar and broken glass, encompassed the
whole. This prisonlike rampart formed the
limit of our domain; beyond it we saw but
thrice a week — once every Saturday afternoon, when, attended by two ushers, we were
permitted to take brief walks in a body
through some of the neighborhood fields —
and twice during Sunday, when we were
paraded in the same formal manner to the
morning and evening service in the one
church of the village. Of this church the
principal of our school was pastor. With how
deep a spirit of wonder and perplexity was I
wont to regard him from our remote pew in
the gallery, as, with step solemn and slow, he

ascended the pulpit! This reverend man, with
countenance so demurely benign, with robes
so glossy and so clerically flowing, with wig
so minutely powdered, so rigid and so vast —
could this be he who, with sour visage, and in
snuffy habiliments, administered, ferule in
hand, the Draconian Laws of the academy?
Oh, gigantic paradox, too utterly monstrous
for solution!

At an angle of the ponderous wall frowned
a more ponderous gate. It was riveted and
studded with iron bolts, and surmounted with
jagged iron spikes. What impressions of deep
awe did it inspire! It was never opened save
for the three periodical egressions and in-
gressions already mentioned; then, in every
creak of its mighty hinges, we found a pleni-
tude of mystery — a world of matter for
solemn remark, or for more solemn meditation.

The extensive enclosure was irregular in
form, having many capacious recesses. Of
these, three or four of the largest constituted
the playground. It was level, and covered
with fine hard gravel. I well remember it had
no trees, nor benches, nor anything similar
within it. Of course it was in the rear of the

house. In front lay a small parterre, planted
with box and other shrubs, but through this
sacred division we passed only upon rare occasions indeed — such as a first advent to
school or final departure thence, or perhaps,
when a parent or friend having called for us,
we joyfully took our way home for the
Christmas or midsummer holidays.

But the house — how quaint an old building was this! — to me how veritably a place
of enchantment! There was really no end to
its windings — to its incomprehensible sub-
divisions. It was difficult, at any given time,
to say with certainty upon which of its two
stories one happened to be. From each room
to every other there were sure to be found
three or four steps either in ascent or descent.
Then the lateral branches were innumerable
— inconceivable — and so returning in upon
themselves that our most exact ideas in regard to the whole mansion were not very far
different from those with which we pondered
upon infinity. During the five years of my
residence here, I was never able to ascertain
with precision in what remote locality lay the
little sleeping apartment assigned to myself
and some eighteen or twenty other scholars.

The schoolroom was the largest in the house — I could not help thinking, in the world. It was very long, narrow, and dismally low, with pointed Gothic windows and a ceiling of oak. In a remote and terror-inspiring angle was a square enclosure of eight or ten feet, comprising the *sanctum*, "during hours," of our principal, the Reverend Dr. Bransby. It was a solid structure, with massy door, sooner than open which in the absence of the "Dominie" we would have willingly perished by the *peine forte et dure*. In other angles were two similar boxes, far less reverenced, indeed, but still greatly matters of awe. One of these was the pulpit of the "classical" usher, one of the "English and mathematical." Interspersed about the room, crossing and recrossing in endless irregularity, were innumerable benches and desks, black, ancient, and time-worn, piled desperately with much bethumbed books, and so beseamed with initial letters, names at full length, grotesque figures, and other multiplied efforts of the knife as to have entirely lost what little of original form might have been their portion in days long departed. A huge bucket with water stood at one extrem-

ity of the room, and a clock of stupendous
dimensions at the other.

Encompassed by the massy walls of this
venerable academy, I passed, yet not in
tedium or disgust, the years of the third
lustrum of my life. The teeming brain of
childhood requires no external world of incident to occupy or amuse it; and the apparently dismal monotony of a school was replete
with more intense excitement than my riper
youth has derived from luxury, or any full
manhood from crime. Yet I must believe that
my first mental development had in it much
of the uncommon — even much of the *outré*.
Upon mankind at large the events of very
early existence rarely leave in mature age any
definite impression. All is gray shadow — a
weak and irregular remembrance — an indistinct regathering of feeble pleasures and
phantasmagoric pains. With me this is not so.
In childhood I must have felt with the energy
of a man what I now find stamped upon
memory in lines as vivid, as deep, and as
durable as the *exergues* of the Carthaginian
medals.

Yet in fact — in the fact of the world's
view — how little was there to remember!

The morning's awakening, the nightly summons to bed; the connings, the recitations; the periodical half-holidays, and perambulations; the playground, with its broils, its pastimes, its intrigues — these, by a mental sorcery long forgotten, were made to involve a wilderness of sensation, a world of rich incident, a universe of varied emotion, of excitement the most passionate and spirit-stirring. *"Oh, le bon temps, que ce siècle de fer!"*

In truth, the ardor, the enthusiasm, and the imperiousness of my disposition soon rendered me a marked character among my schoolmates, and by slow, but natural gradations, gave me an ascendancy over all not greatly older than myself — over all with a single exception. This exception was found in the person of a scholar, who, although no relation, bore the same Christian and surname as myself — a circumstance, in fact, little remarkable; for, notwithstanding a noble descent, mine was one of those every-day appellations which seem, by prescriptive right, to have been, time out of mind, the common property of the mob. In this narrative I have therefore designated myself as

William Wilson — a fictitious title not very
dissimilar to the real. My namesake alone, of
those who in school phraseology constituted
"our set," presumed to compete with me in
the studies of the class, in the sports and
broils of the playground, to refuse implicit
belief in my assertions, and submission to
my will — indeed, to interfere with my arbitrary dictation in any respect whatsoever. If
there is on earth a supreme and unqualified
despotism, it is the despotism of a master
mind in boyhood over the less energetic
spirits of its companions.

Wilson's rebellion was to me a source of
the greatest embarrassment; the more so as,
in spite of the bravado with which in public
I made a point of treating him and his pre-
tensions, I secretly felt that I feared him, and
could not help thinking the equality which he
maintained so easily with myself a proof of
his true superiority, since not to be overcome
cost me a perpetual struggle. Yet this
superiority — even this equality — was in
truth acknowledged by no one but myself; our
associates, by some unaccountable blindness,
seemed not even to suspect it. Indeed, his
competition, his resistance, and especially his

impertinent and dogged interference with my purposes were not more pointed than private. He appeared to be destitute alike of the ambition which urged and of the passionate energy of mind which enabled me to excel. In his rivalry he might have been supposed actuated solely by a whimsical desire to thwart, astonish, or mortify myself; although there were times when I could not help observing, with a feeling made up of wonder, abasement, and pique, that he mingled with his injuries, his insults, or his contradictions, a certain most inappropriate and assuredly most unwelcome *affectionateness* of manner. I could only conceive this singular behavior to arise from a consummate self-conceit assuming vulgar airs of patronage and protection.

Perhaps it was this latter trait in Wilson's conduct, conjoined with our identity of name and the mere accident of our having entered the school upon the same day, which set afloat the notion that we were brothers, among the senior classes in the academy. These do not usually inquire with much strictness into the affairs of their juniors. I have before said, or should have said, that

Wilson was not, in a most remote degree, connected with my family. But assuredly if we *had* been brothers we must have been twins; for, after leaving Dr. Bransby's I casually learned that my namesake was born on the nineteenth of January, 1813 — and this is a somewhat remarkable coincidence, for the day is precisely that of my own nativity.

It may seem strange that in spite of the continual anxiety occasioned me by the rivalry of Wilson and his intolerable spirit of contradiction, I could not bring myself to hate him altogether. We had, to be sure, nearly every day a quarrel in which, yielding me publicly the palm of victory, he, in some manner, contrived to make me feel that it was he who had deserved it; yet a sense of pride on my part, and a vertible dignity on his own, kept us always upon what are called "speaking terms," while there were many points of strong congeniality in our tempers, operating to awake in me a sentiment which our position alone, perhaps, prevented from ripening into friendship. It is difficult, indeed, to define, or even to describe, my real feelings toward him. They formed a motley and heterogeneous admixture — some petulant animosity, which was not yet hatred; some esteem, more respect, much fear, with a world of uneasy curiosity. To the moralist it will be necessary to say, in addition, that Wilson and myself were the most inseparable of companions.

It was no doubt the anomalous state of affairs existing between us which turned all my attacks upon him (and there were many, either open or covert) into the channel of banter or practical joke (giving pain while assuming the aspect of mere fun), rather than into a more serious and determined hostility. But my endeavors on this head were by no means uniformly successful, even when my plans were the most wittily concocted; for my namesake had much about him, in character, of that unassuming and quiet austerity which, while enjoying the poignancy of its own jokes, has no heel of Achilles in itself, and absolutely refuses to be laughed at. I could find, indeed, but one vulnerable point, and that, lying in a personal peculiarity, arising, perhaps, from constitutional disease, would have been spared by any antagonist less at his wit's end than myself — my rival had a weakness in the faucal or guttural

organs, which precluded him from raising his
voice at any time *above a very low whisper*.
Of this defect I did not fail to take what poor
advantage lay in my power.

Wilson's retaliations in kind were many;
and there was one form of his practical wit
that disturbed me beyond measure. How his
sagacity first discovered at all that so petty
a thing would vex me is a question I never
could solve; but having discovered, he habitually practiced the annoyance. I had always
felt aversion to my uncourtly patronymic and
its very common, if not plebeian, prenomen.
The words were venom in my ears; and when,
upon the day of my arrival, a second William
Wilson came also to the academy, I felt angry
with him for bearing the name, and doubly
disgusted with the name because a stranger
bore it, who would be the cause of its two-fold
repetition, who would be constantly in my
presence, and whose concerns, in the ordinary
routine of the school business, must inevitably, on account of the detestable coincidence, be often confounded with my own.

The feeling of vexation thus engendered
grew stronger with every circumstance tending to show resemblance, moral or physical,

between my rival and myself. I had not then
discovered the remarkable fact that we were
of the same age; but I saw that we were of
the same height, and I perceived that we were
even singularly alike in general contour of
person and outline of feature. I was galled,
too, by the rumor touching a relationship,
which had grown current in the upper forms.
In a word, nothing could more seriously dis-
turb me (although I scrupulously concealed
such disturbance) than any allusion to a
similarity of mind, person, or condition existing between us. But, in truth, I had no reason
to believe that (with the exception of the
matter of relationship, and in the case of
Wilson himself) this similarity had ever been
made a subject of comment, or even observed
at all by our schoolfellows. That *he* observed
it in all its bearings and as fixedly as I, was
apparent; but that he could discover in such
circumstances so fruitful a field of annoyance
can only be attributed, as I said before, to his
more than ordinary penetration.

His cue, which was to perfect an imitation
of myself, lay both in words and in actions;
and most admirably did he play his part. My
dress it was an easy matter to copy; my gait

and general manner were without difficulty appropriated; in spite of his constitutional defect, even my voice did not escape him. My louder tones were, of course, unattempted, but then the key — it was identical; *and his singular whisper, it grew the very echo of my own.*

How greatly this most exquisite portraiture harassed me (for it could not justly be termed a caricature), I will not now venture to describe. I had but one consolation — in the fact that the imitation, apparently, was noticed by myself alone, and that I had to endure only the knowing and strangely sarcastic smiles of my namesake himself. Satisfied with having produced in my bosom the intended effect, he seemed to chuckle in secret over the sting he had inflicted, and was characteristically disregardful of the public applause which the success of his witty endeavors might have so easily elicited. That the school, indeed, did not feel his design, perceive its accomplishment, and participate in his sneer was, for many anxious months, a riddle I could not resolve. Perhaps the *gradation* of his copy rendered it not readily perceptible; or, more possibly, I owed my

security to the masterly air of the copyist,
who, disdaining the letter (which in a painting is all the obtuse can see), gave but the full
spirit of his original for my individual contemplation and chagrin.

I have already more than once spoken of
the disgusting air of patronage which he
assumed toward me, and of his frequent
officious interference with my will. This interference often took the ungracious character of advice; advice not openly given, but
hinted or insinuated. I received it with a re-
pugnance which gained strength as I grew in
years. Yet, at this distant day, let me do him
the simple justice to acknowledge that I can
recall no occasion when the suggestions of my
rival were on the side of those errors or
follies so usual to his immature age and
seeming inexperience; that his moral sense,
at least, if not his general talents and worldly
wisdom, was far keener than my own; and
that I might, today, have been a better and
thus a happier man had I less frequently rejected the counsels embodied in those meaning whispers which I then but too cordially
hated and too bitterly despised.

As it was I at length grew restive in the

extreme under his distasteful supervision, and daily resented more and more openly what I considered his intolerable arrogance. I have said that, in the first years of our connection as schoolmates, my feelings in regard to him might have been easily ripened into friendship; but, in the latter months of my residence at the academy, although the intrusion of his ordinary manner had, beyond doubt, in some measure abated, my sentiments, in nearly similar proportion, partook very much of positive hatred. Upon one occasion he saw this, I think, and afterward avoided, or made a show of avoiding me.

It was about the same period, if I remember aright, that, in an altercation of violence with him, in which he was more than usually thrown off his guard, and spoke and acted with an openness of demeanor rather foreign to his nature, I discovered, or fancied I discovered, in his accent, in his air and general appearance, a something which first startled, and then deeply interested me, by bringing to mind dim visions of my earliest infancy — wild, confused, and thronging memories of a time when memory herself was yet unborn. I cannot better describe the sensation which

oppressed me than by saying that I could with
difficulty shake off the belief of my having
been acquainted with the being who stood before me, at some epoch very long ago — some
point of the past even infinitely remote. The
delusion, however, faded rapidly as it came;
and I mention it at all but to define the day
of the last conversation I there held with my
singular namesake.

The huge old house, with its countless sub-
divisions, had several large chambers com-
municating with each other, where slept the
greater number of the students. There were,
however (as must necessarily happen in a
building so awkwardly planned), many little
nooks or recesses, the odds and ends of the
structure; and these the economic ingenuity
of Dr. Bransby had also fitted up as dormi-
tories; although, being the merest closets,
they were capable of accommodating but a
single individual. One of these small apartments was occupied by Wilson.

One night, about the close of my fifth year
at the school, and immediately after the altercation just mentioned, finding everyone
wrapped in sleep, I arose from bed, and, lamp
in hand, stole through a wilderness of narrow

passages from my own bedroom to that of my
rival. I had long been plotting one of those
ill-natured pieces of practical wit at his expense in which I had hitherto been so uniformly unsuccessful. It was my intention,
now, to put my scheme in operation, and I
resolved to make him feel the whole extent of
the malice with which I was imbued. Having
reached his closet, I noiselessly entered, leaving the lamp, with a shade over it, on the
outside. I advanced a step and listened to the
sound of his tranquil breathing. Assured of
his being asleep, I returned, took the light,
and with it again approached the bed. Close
curtains were around it, which, in the prosecution of my plan, I slowly and quietly with-
drew, when the bright rays fell vividly upon
the sleeper, and my eyes at the same moment
upon his countenance. I looked — and a
numbness, an iciness of feeling instantly pervaded my frame. My breast heaved, my knees
tottered, my whole spirit became possessed
with an objectless yet intolerable horror.
Gasping for breath, I lowered the lamp in
still nearer proximity to the face. Were these
— *these* the lineaments of William Wilson? I
saw, indeed, that they were his, but I shook

as if with a fit of the ague, in fancying they were not. What *was* there about them to confound me in this manner? I gazed, while my brain reeled with a multitude of incoherent thoughts. Not thus he appeared — assuredly not *thus* — in the vivacity of his waking hours. The same name! the same contour of person! the same day of arrival at the academy! And then his dogged and meaningless imitation of my gait, my voice, my habits, and my manner! Was it, in truth, within the bounds of human possibility that *what I now saw* was the result, merely, of the habitual practice of this sarcastic imitation? Awe-stricken, and with a creeping shudder, I extinguished the lamp, passed silently from the chamber, and left, at once, the halls of that old academy, never to enter them again.

After a lapse of some months, spent at home in mere idleness, I found myself a student at Eton. The brief interval had been sufficient to enfeeble my remembrance of the events at Dr. Bransby's, or at least to effect a material change in the nature of the feelings with which I remembered them. The truth — the tragedy — of the drama was no more. I could now find room to doubt the evidence of my senses; and seldom called up the subject at all but with wonder at the extent of human credulity, and a smile at the vivid force of the imagination which I hereditarily possessed. Neither was this species of skepticism likely to be diminished by the character of the life I led at Eton. The vortex of thoughtless folly into which I there so immediately and so recklessly plunged washed away all but the froth of my past hours, ingulfed at once every solid or serious impression, and left to memory only the veriest levities of a former existence.

I do not wish, however, to trace the course of my miserable profligacy here — a profligacy which set at defiance the laws, while it eluded the vigilance of the institution. Three years of folly, passed without profit, had but given me rooted habits of vice, and added, in a somewhat unusual degree, to my bodily stature, when, after a week of soulless dissipation, I invited a small party of the most dissolute students to a secret carousal in my chambers. We met at a late hour of the night, for our debaucheries were to be faithfully protracted until morning. The wine flowed freely, and there were not wanting other and

perhaps more dangerous seductions; so that
the gray dawn had already faintly appeared
in the east while our delirious extravagance
was at its height. Madly flushed with cards
and intoxication, I was in the act of insisting
upon a toast of more than wonted profanity
when my attention was suddenly diverted by
the violent, although partial, unclosing of the
door of the apartment, and by the eager voice
of a servant from without. He said that some
person, apparently in great haste, demanded
to speak with me in the hall.

Wildly excited with wine, the unexpected
interruptions rather delighted than surprised
me. I staggered forward at once, and a few
steps brought me to the vestibule of the building. In this low and small room there hung no
lamp; and now no light at all was admitted,
save that of the exceedingly feeble dawn
which made its way through the semicircu-
lar window. As I put my foot over the
threshold, I became aware of the figure of a
youth about my own height, and habited in a
white kerseymere morning frock, cut in the
novel fashion of the one I myself wore at the
moment. This the faint light enabled me to
perceive; but the features of his face I could

not distinguish. Upon my entering, he strode hurriedly up to me, and, seizing me by the arm with a gesture of petulant impatience, whispered the words "William Wilson" in my ear.

I grew perfectly sober in an instant.

There was that in the manner of the stranger, and in the tremulous shake of his uplifted finger, as he held it between my eyes and the light, which filled me with unqualified amazement; but it was not this which had so violently moved me. It was the pregnancy of solemn admonition in the singular low, hissing utterance; and, above all, it was the character, the tone, *the key*, of those few, simple, and familiar, yet *whispered* syllables, which came with a thousand thronging memories of bygone days, and struck upon my soul with the shock of a galvanic battery. Ere I could recover the use of my senses he was gone.

Although this event failed not of a vivid effect upon my disordered imagination, yet was it evanescent as vivid. For some weeks, indeed, I busied myself in earnest inquiry, or was wrapped in a cloud of morbid speculation. I did not pretend to disguise from my

perception the identity of the singular individual who thus perseveringly interfered
with my affairs and harassed me with his
insinuated counsel. But who and what was
this Wilson? — and whence came he? — and
what were his purposes? Upon neither of
these points could I be satisfied — merely
ascertaining, in regard to him, that a sudden
accident in his family had caused his removal
from Dr. Bransby's academy on the afternoon of the day in which I myself had eloped.
But in a brief period I ceased to think upon
the subject, my attention being all absorbed
in a contemplated departure for Oxford.
Thither I soon went, the uncalculating vanity
of my parents furnishing me with an outfit
and annual establishment, which would enable me to indulge at will in the luxury so
dear to my heart — to vie in profuseness of
expenditure with the haughtiest heirs of the
wealthiest earldoms in Great Britain.

Excited by such appliances to vice, my
constitutional temperament broke forth with
redoubled ardor, and I spurned even the common restraints of decency in the mad infatua-
tion of my revels. But it were absurd to pause
in the detail of my extravagance. Let it

suffice, that among spendthrifts I out-Heroded Herod, and that, giving name to a multitude of novel follies, I added no brief appendix to the long catalogue of vices then usual in the most dissolute university of Europe.

It could hardly be credited, however, that I had, even here, so utterly fallen from the gentlemanly estate as to seek acquaintance with the vilest arts of the gambler by profession, and, having become an adept in his despicable science, to practice it habitually as a means of increasing my already enormous income at the expense of the weak-minded among my fellow collegians. Such, nevertheless, was the fact. And the very enormity of this offense against all manly and honorable sentiment proved, beyond doubt, the main if not the sole reason of the impunity with which it was committed. Who, indeed, among my most abandoned associates, would not rather have disputed the clearest evidence of his senses than have suspected of such courses the gay, the frank, the generous William Wilson — the noblest and most liberal commoner at Oxford — him whose follies (said his parasites) were but the

follies of youth and unbridled fancy — whose
errors but inimitable whim — whose darkest
vice but a careless and dashing extravagance?

I had been now two years successfully
busied in this way when there came to the
university a young *parvenu* nobleman,
Glendinning — rich, said report, as Herodes
Atticus — his riches, too, as easily acquired.
I soon found him of weak intellect, and, of
course, marked him as a fitting subject for
my skill. I frequently engaged him in play,
and contrived, with the gambler's usual art,
to let him win considerable sums, the more
effectually to entangle him in my snares. At
length, my schemes being ripe, I met him
(with the full intention that this meeting
should be final and decisive) at the chamber
of a fellow commoner (Mr. Preston), equally
intimate with both, but who, to do him justice, entertained not even a remote suspicion
of my design. To give to this a better coloring, I had contrived to have assembled a
party of some eight or ten, and was solicit-
ously careful that the introduction of cards
should appear accidental, and originate in
the proposal of my contemplated dupe himself. To be brief upon a vile topic, none of

the low finesse was omitted, so customary upon similar occasions, that it is a just matter for wonder how any are still found so besotted as to fall its victim.

We had protracted our sitting far into the night, and I had at length affected the maneuver of getting Glendinning as my sole antagonist. The game, too, was my favorite *écarté*. The rest of the company, interested in the extent of our play, had abandoned their own cards and were standing around us as spectators. The *parvenu*, who had been induced by my artifices in the early part of the evening, to drink deeply, now shuffled, dealt, or played, with a wild nervousness of manner for which his intoxication, I thought, might partially, but could not altogether, account. In a very short period he had become my debtor to a large amount, when, having taken a long draught of port, he did precisely what I had been coolly anticipating — he proposed to double our already extravagant stakes. With a well-feigned show of reluctance, and not until after my repeated refusal had seduced him into some angry words which gave a color of *pique* to my compliance, did I finally comply. The result, of course, did but

prove entirely the prey was in my toils: in
less than an hour he had quadrupled his debt.
For some time his countenance had been
losing the florid tinge lent it by the wine; but
now, to my astonishment, I perceived that it
had grown to a pallor truly fearful. I say, to
my astonishment. Glendinning had been
represented to my eager inquiries as im-
measurably wealthy: and the sums which he
had as yet lost, although in themselves vast,
could not, I supposed, very seriously annoy,
much less so violently affect him. That he was
overcome by the wine just swallowed was the
idea which most readily presented itself; and,
rather with a view to the preservation of my
own character in the eyes of my associates,
than from any less interested motive, I was
about to insist, peremptorily, upon a discon-
tinuance of the play, when some expressions
at my elbow from among the company, and
an ejaculation evincing utter despair on the
part of Glendinning, gave me to understand
that I had effected his total ruin under circumstances which, rendering him an object
for the pity of all, should have protected him
from the ill offices even of a fiend.

What now might have been my conduct it

is difficult to say. The pitiable condition of my dupe had thrown an air of embarrassed gloom over all; and, for some moments, a profound silence was maintained, during which I could not help feeling my cheeks tingled with the many burning glances of scorn or reproach cast upon me by the less abandoned of the party. I will even own that an intolerable weight of anxiety was for a brief instant lifted from my bosom by the sudden and extraordinary interruption which ensued. The wide, heavy folding doors of the apartment were all at once thrown open, to their full extent, with a vigorous and rushing impetuosity that extinguished, as if by magic, every candle in the room. Their light, in dying, enable us to perceive that a stranger had entered, about my own height, and closely muffled in a cloak. The darkness, however, was not total; and we could only *feel* that he was standing in our midst. Before any one of us could recover from the extreme astonishment into which this rudeness had thrown all, we heard the voice of the intruder.

"Gentlemen," he said, in a low, distinct, and never-to-be-forgotten *whisper* which thrilled to the very marrow of my bones, "Gentlemen, I make an apology for this behavior, because in thus behaving, I am fulfilling a duty. You are, beyond doubt, uninformed of the true character of the person who has tonight won at *écarté* a large sum of money from Lord Glendinning. I will therefore put you upon an expeditious and decisive plan of obtaining this very necessary information. Please to examine, at your leisure, the inner linings of the cuff of his left sleeve, and the several little packages which may be found in the somewhat capacious pockets of his embroidered morning wrapper."

While he spoke, so profound was the stillness that one might have heard a pin drop upon the floor. In ceasing, he departed at once, and as abruptly as he had entered. Can I — shall I describe my sensations? Must I say that I felt all the horrors of the damned? Most assuredly I had little time for reflection. Many hands roughly seized me upon the spot, and lights were immediately reprocured. A search ensued. In the lining of my sleeve were found all the court cards essential in *écarté*, and in the pockets of my wrapper, a number of packs, facsimiles of those used at our sittings, with the single exception that mine were of the species called, technically, *arrondees;* the honors being slightly convex at the ends, the lower cards slightly convex at the sides. In this disposition, the dupe who cuts, as customary, at the length of the pack, will invariably find that he cuts his antagonist an honor; while the gambler, cutting at the breadth, will, as certainly, cut nothing for his victim which may count in the records of the game.

Any burst of indignation upon this discovery would have affected me less than the silent contempt, or the sarcastic composure, with which it was received.

"Mr. Wilson," said our host, stooping to remove from beneath his feet an exceedingly luxurious cloak of rare furs, "Mr. Wilson, this is your property." (The weather was cold; and, upon quitting my own room, I had thrown a cloak over my dressing wrapper, putting it off upon reaching the scene of play.) "I presume it is supererogatory to seek here (eyeing the folds of the garment with a bitter smile) for any farther evidence of your skill. Indeed, we have had enough. You will see the necessity, I hope, of quitting Oxford

— at all events, of quitting instantly my chambers."

Abased, humbled to the dust as I then was, it is probable that I should have resented this galling language by immediate personal violence, had not my whole attention been at the moment arrested by a fact of the most startling character. The cloak which I had worn was of a rare description of fur; how rare, how extravagantly costly, I shall not venture to say. Its fashion, too, was of my own fantastic invention: for I was fastidious to an absurd degree of coxcombry in matters of this frivolous nature. When, therefore, Mr. Preston reached me that which he had picked up upon the floor, and near the folding doors of the apartment, it was with an astonishment nearly bordering upon terror that I perceived my own already hanging on my arm (where I had no doubt unwittingly placed it), and that the one presented me was but its exact counterpart in every, in even the minutest possible particular. The singular being who had so disastrously exposed me had been muffled, I remembered, in a cloak; and none had been worn at all by any of the memebers of our party, with the exception of myself. Retaining some presence of mind, I took the one offered me by Preston; placed it, unnoticed, over my own; left the apartment with a resolute scowl of defiance; and, next morning ere dawn of day, commenced a hurried journey from Oxford to the continent, in a perfect agony of horror and of shame.

I fled in vain. My evil destiny pursued me as if in exultation, and proved, indeed. that the exercise of its mysterious dominion had as yet only begun. Scarcely had I set foot in Paris, ere I had fresh evidence of the detestable interest taken by this Wilson in my concerns. Years flew, while I experienced no relief. Villain! — at Rome, with how untimely. yet with how spectral an officiousness, stepped he in between me and my ambition! at Vienna, too — at Berlin — and at Moscow! Where, in truth. had I *not* bitter cause to curse him within my heart? From his inscrutable tyranny did I at length flee, panic-stricken, as from a pestilence; and to the very ends of the earth *I fled in vain.*

And again, and again, in secret communion with my own spirit, would I demand the questions "Who is he? — whence came he? —

and what are his objects?" But no answer
was there found. And now I scrutinized, with
a minute scrutiny, the forms, and the
methods, and the leading traits of his impertinent supervision. But even here there
was very little upon which to base a conjec-
ture. It was noticeable, indeed, that, in no one
of the multiplied instances in which he had of
late crossed my path, had he so crossed it
except to frustrate those schemes, or to dis-
turb those actions, which, if fully carried out,
might have resulted in bitter mischief. Poor
justification this, in truth, for an authority
so imperiously assumed! Poor indemnity for
natural rights of self-agency so pertinaciously, so insultingly denied!

I had also been forced to notice that my
tormentor, for a very long period of time,
(while scrupulously and with miraculous
dexterity maintaining his whim of an identity of apparel with myself,) had so contrived
it, in the execution of his varied interference
with my will, that I saw not, at any moment,
the features of his face. Be Wilson what he
might, *this* at least, was but the veriest of
affectation, or of folly. Could he, for an instant, have supposed that, in my admonisher

at Eton — in the destroyer of my honor at Oxford — in him who thwarted my ambition at Rome, my revenge at Paris, my passionate love at Naples, or what he falsely termed my avarice in Egypt — that in this, my arch-enemy and evil genius, I could fail to recognize the William Wilson of my schoolboy days — the namesake, the companion, the rival — the hated and dreaded rival at Bransby's? Impossible! — But let me hasten to the last eventful scene of the drama.

Thus far I had succumbed supinely to this imperious domination. The sentiment of deep awe with which I habitually regarded the elevated character, the majestic wisdom, the apparent omnipresence and omnipotence of Wilson, added to a feeling of even terror, with which certain other traits in his nature and assumptions inspired me, had operated, hitherto, to impress me with an idea of my own utter weakness and helplessness, and to suggest an implicit, although bitterly reluctant submission to his arbitrary will. But, of late days, I had given myself up entirely to wine; and its maddening influence upon my hereditary temper rendered me more and more impatient of control. I began to mur-

mur, to hesitate, to resist. And was it only
fancy which induced me to believe that, with
the increase of my own firmness, that of my
tormentor underwent a proportional diminu-
tion? Be this as it may, I now began to feel
the inspiration of a burning hope, and at
length nurtured in my secret thoughts a stern
and desperate resolution that I would submit
no longer to be enslaved.

It was at Rome, during the Carnival of
18—, that I attended a masquerade in the
palazzo of the Neapolitan Duke Di Broglio.
I had indulged more freely than usual in the
excesses of the wine table; and now the suffo-
cating atmosphere of the crowded rooms
irritated me beyond endurance. The difficulty,
too, of forcing my way through the mazes of
the company contributed not a little to the
ruffling of my temper; for I was anxiously
seeking (let me not say with what unworthy
motive) the young, the gay, the beautiful
wife of the aged and doting Di Broglio. With
a too unscrupulous confidence she had previously communicated to me the secret of the
costume in which she would be habited, and
now, having caught a glimpse of her person,
I was hurrying to make my way into her

presence. At this moment I felt a light hand placed upon my shoulder, and that ever-remembered, low, damnable *whisper* within my ear.

In an absolute frenzy of wrath, I turned at once upon him who had thus interrupted me, and seized him violently by the collar. He was attired, as I had expected, in a costume altogether similar to my own; wearing a Spanish cloak of blue velvet, begirt about the waist with a crimson belt sustaining a rapier. A mask of black silk entirely covered his face.

"Scoundrel!" I said, in a voice husky with rage, while every syllable I uttered seemed as new fuel to my fury. "Scoundrel! imposter! accursed villain! You shall not — you *shall not* dog me unto death! Follow me, or I stab you where you stand!" — and I broke my way from the ballroom into a small antechamber adjoining, dragging him unresistingly with me as I went.

Upon entering, I thrust him furiously from me. He staggered against the wall, while I closed the door with an oath, and commanded him to draw. He hesitated but for an instant; then, with a slight sigh, drew in silence, and put himself upon the defense.

The contest was brief indeed. I was frantic with every species of wild excitement, and felt within my single arm the energy and power of a multitude. In a few seconds I forced him by sheer strength against the wainscotting, and thus, getting him at mercy, plunged my sword, with brute ferocity, repeatedly through and through his bosom.

At that instant some person tried the latch of the door. I hastened to prevent an intrusion, and then immediately returned to my dying antagonist. But what human language can adequately portray *that* astonishment, *that* horror which possessed me at the spectacle then presented to view? The brief moment in which I averted my eyes had been sufficient to produce, apparently, a material change in the arrangements at the upper or farther end of the room. A large mirror — so at first it seemed to me in my confusion — now stood where none had been perceptible before; and as I stepped up to it in extremity of terror, mine own image, but with features all pale and dabbled in blood, advanced to meet me with a feeble and tottering gait.

Thus it appeared, I say, but was not. It was my antagonist — it was Wilson, who then stood before me in the agonies of his dissolution. His mask and cloak lay, where he had thrown them, upon the floor. Not a thread in all his raiment — not a line in all the marked and singular lineaments of his face which was not, even in the most absolute identity, *mine own!*

It was Wilson; but he spoke no longer in a whisper, and I could have fancied that I myself was speaking while he said:

"You have conquered, and I yield. Yet henceforward art thou also dead — dead to the World, to Heaven, and to Hope! In me didst thou exist — and, in my death, see by this image, which is thine own, how utterly thou hast murdered thyself."

The Masque
of the
Red Death

This most pictorial of Poe's prose writings appeared in *Graham's Magazine* for May, 1842. Poe does not exaggerate the horror of cholera, which, says Paul de Kruif, "sneaked into healthy men in the morning, doubled them into knots of spasm-racked agony by afternoon, and put them to rest beyond the reach of all pain by night." Poe himself had lived through an epidemic of cholera and had seen the symptoms with his own eyes. Some may think of the story as a warning to the man who indulges his private pleasures while the rest of the world is racked with disease. Or, the story may have no other purpose than to foreshadow and accomplish the end of Prospero and his "thousand friends." Whatever we think about its meaning (and it may have none at all), we cannot ignore the imagery and symbolism — the blood-red windows of the seventh apartment, the dream quality of the dancers, the deep voice of the striking clock with its reminder of mortality ("three thousand and six hundred seconds of the Time that flies"). Of all the Poe tales, this is the best one to read aloud.

The "Red Death" had long devastated the country. No pestilence had ever been so fatal, or so hideous. Blood was its Avatar and its seal — the redness and the horror of blood. There were sharp pains, and sudden dizziness, and then profuse bleeding at the pores, with dissolution. The scarlet stains upon the body and especially upon the face of the victim, were the pest ban which shut him out from the aid and from the sympathy of his fellow men. And the whole siezure, progress, and termination of the disease were the incidents of half an hour.

But the Prince Prospero was happy and dauntless and sagacious. When his dominions were half depopulated, he summoned to his presence a thousand hale and light-hearted friends from among the knights and dames of his court, and with these retired to the deep seclusion of one of his castellated abbeys. This was an extensive and magnificent structure, the creation of the prince's own eccentric yet august taste. A strong and lofty wall girdled it in. This wall had gates of iron. The courtiers, having entered, brought furnaces and massy hammers and welded the bolts. They resolved to leave means neither of ingress nor egress t othe sudden impulses of despair or of frenzy from within. The abbey was amply provisioned. With such precautions the courtiers might bid defiance to contagion. The external world could take care of itself. In the meantime it was folly to grieve, or to think. The prince had provided all the appliances of pleasure. There were buffoons, there were improvisators, there were ballet dancers, there were musicians, there was Beauty, there was wine. All these and security were within. Without was the "Red Death."

It was toward the close of the fifth or sixth month of his seclusion, and while the pestilence raged most furiously abroad, that the Prince Prospero entertained his thousand friends at a masked ball of the most unusual magnificence.

It was a voluptuous scene, that masquerade. But first let me tell of the rooms in which it was held. There were seven — an imperial suite. In many palaces, however, such suites form a long and straight vista, while the folding doors slide back nearly to the walls on either hand, so that the view of the whole extent is scarcely impeded. Here the case was very different, as might have been expected from the duke's love of the bizarre. The apartments were so irregularly disposed that the vision embraced but little more than one at a time. There was a sharp turn at every twenty or thirty yards, and at each turn a novel effect. To the right and left, in the middle of each wall, a tall and narrow Gothic window looked out upon a closed corridor which pursued the windings of the suite. These windows were of stained glass whose color varied in accordance with the prevailing hue of the decorations of the chamber into which it opened. That at the eastern extremity was hung, for example, in blue — and vividly blue were its windows. The second chamber was purple in its ornaments and tapestries, and here the panes were purple. The third was green throughout, and so were the casements. The fourth was fur-

nished and lighted with orange — the fifth
with white — the sixth with violet. The
seventh apartment was closely shrouded in
black-velvet tapestries that hung all over the
ceiling and down the walls, falling in heavy
folds upon a carpet of the same materials and
hue. But in this chamber only, the color of the
windows failed to correspond with the decorations. The panes here were scarlet — a deep
blood color. Now in no one of the seven
apartments was there any lamp or candela-
brum, amid the profusion of golden ornaments that lay scattered to and fro or
depended from the roof. There was no light
of any kind emanating from lamp or candle
within the suite of chambers. But in the cor-
ridors that followed the suite, there stood,
opposite to each window, a heavy tripod,
bearing a brazier of fire, that projected its
rays through the tinted glass and so glaringly
illumined the room. And thus were produced
a multitude of gaudy and fantastic appearances. But in the western or black chamber
the effect of the firelight that streamed upon
the dark hangings through the blood-tinted
panes was ghastly in the extreme, and produced so wild a look upon the countenances
of those who entered that there were few of

the company bold enough to set foot within
its precincts at all.

It was in this apartment, also, that there
stood against the western wall, a gigantic
clock of ebony. Its pendulum swung to and
fro with a dull, heavy, monotonous clang; and
when the minute hand made the circuit of the
face, and the hour was to be stricken, there
came from the brazen lungs of the clock a
sound which was clear and loud and deep and
exceedingly musical, but of so peculiar a note
and emphasis that, at each lapse of an hour,
the musicians of the orchestra were constrained to pause, momentarily, in their per-
formance, to hearken to the sound; and thus
the waltzers perforce ceased their evolutions;
and there was a brief disconcert of the whole
gay company; and, while the chimes of the
clock yet rang, it was observed that the
giddiest grew pale, and the more aged and
sedate passed their hands over their brows
as if in confused revery or meditation. But
when the echoes had fully ceased, a light
laughter at once pervaded the assembly; the
musicians looked at each other and smiled as
if at their own nervousness and folly, and
made whispering vows, each to the other,
that the next chiming of the clock should

produce in them no similar emotion; and then, after the lapse of sixty minutes (which embrace three thousand and six hundred seconds of the Time that flies), there came yet another chiming of the clock, and then were the same disconcert and tremulousness and meditation as before.

But, in spite of these things, it was a gay and magnificent revel. The tastes of the duke were peculiar. He had a fine eye for colors and effects. He disregarded the *decora* of mere fashion. His plans were bold and fiery, and his conceptions glowed with barbaric luster. There are some who would have thought him mad. His followers felt that he was not. It was necessary to hear and see and touch him to be *sure* that he was not.

He had directed, in great part, the movable embellishments of the seven chambers, upon occasion of this great *fête;* and it was his own guiding taste which had given character to the masqueraders. Be sure they were grotesque. There were much glare and glitter and piquancy and phantasm — much of what has been since seen in *Hernani.* There were arabesque figures with unsuited limbs and appointments. There were delirious fancies such as the madman fashions. There were much of the beautiful, much of the wanton, much of the bizarre, something of the terrible, and not a little of that which might have excited disgust. To and fro in the seven chambers there stalked, in fact, a multitude of dreams. And these — the dreams — writhed in and about, taking hue from the rooms, and causing the wild music of the orchestra to seem as the echo of their steps. And, anon, there strikes the ebony clock which stands in the hall of the velvet. And then, for a moment, all is still, and all is silent save the voice of the clock. The dreams are stiff-frozen as they stand. But the echoes of the chime die away — they have endured but an instant — and a light, half-subdued laughter floats after them as they depart. And now again the music swells, and the dreams live, and writhe to and fro more merrily than ever, taking hue from the many-tinted windows through which stream the rays from the tripods. But to the chamber which lies most westwardly of the seven there are now none of the maskers who venture; for the night is waning away; and there flows a ruddier light through the blood-colored panes; and the blackness of the sable drapery appalls; and to him whose foot falls

upon the sable carpet, there comes from the
near clock of ebony a muffled peal more
solemnly emphatic than any which reaches
their ears who indulge in the more remote
gaieties of the other apartments.

But these other apartments were densely
crowded, and in them beat feverishly the
heart of life. And the revel went whirlingly
on, until at length there commenced the sound-
ing of midnight upon the clock. And then the
music ceased, as I have told; and the evolutions of the waltzers were quieted; and there
was an uneasy cessation of all things as before. But now there were twelve strokes to be
sounded by the bell of the clock; and thus it
happened, perhaps that more of thought
crept, with more of time, into the meditations
of the thoughtful among those who reveled.
And thus too, it happened, perhaps, that before the last echoes of the last chime had
utterly sunk into silence, there were many
individuals in the crowd who had found
leisure to become aware of the presence of a
masked figure which had arrested the attention of no single individual before. And the
rumor of this new presence having spread
itself whisperingly around, there arose at

length from the whole company a buzz, or
murmur, expressive of disapprobation and
surprise — then, finally, of terror, of horror,
and of disgust.

In an assembly of phantasms such as I
have painted, it may well be supposed that no
ordinary appearance could have excited such
sensation. In truth the masquerade license of
the night was nearly unlimited; but the
figure in question had out-Heroded Herod,
and gone beyond the bounds of even the
prince's indefinite decorum. There are chords
in the hearts of the most reckless which cannot be touched without emotion. Even with
the utterly lost, to whom life and death are
equally jests, there are matters of which no
jest can be made. The whole company, indeed,
seemed now deeply to feel that in the costume
and bearing of the stranger neither wit nor
propriety existed. The figure was tall and
gaunt, and shrouded from head to foot in the
habiliments of the grave. The mask which
concealed the visage was made so nearly to
resemble the countenance of a stiffened
corpse that the closest scrutiny must have
had difficulty in detecting the cheat. And yet
all this might have been endured, if not

approved, by the mad revelers around. But the mummer had gone so far as to assume the type of the Red Death. His vesture was dabbled in *blood* — and his broad brow, with all the features of the face, was besprinkled with the scarlet horror.

When the eyes of Prince Prospero fell upon this spectral image (which, with a slow and solemn movement, as if more fully to sustain its *rôle*, stalked to and fro among the waltzers), he was seen to be convulsed, in the first moment with a strong shudder either of terror or distaste; but, in the next, his brow reddened with rage.

"Who dares," he demanded hoarsely of the courtiers who stood near him, "who dares insult us with this blasphemous mockery? Seize him and unmask him — that we may know whom we have to hang, at sunrise, from the battlements!"

It was in the eastern or blue chamber in which stood the Prince Prospero as he uttered these words. They rang throughout the seven rooms loudly and clearly, for the prince was a bold and robust man, and the music had become hushed at the waving of his hand.

It was in the blue room where stood the prince, with a group of pale courtiers by his

side. At first, as he spoke, there was a slight
rushing movement of this group in the direction of the intruder, who, at the moment was
also near at hand, and now, with deliberate
and stately step, made closer approach to the
speaker. But from a certain nameless awe
with which the mad assumptions of the mummer had inspired the whole party, there were
found none who put forth hand to seize him;
so that, unimpeded, he passed within a yard
of the prince's person; and, while the vast
assembly, as if with one impulse, shrank
from the centers of the rooms to the walls, he
made his way uninterruptedly, but with the
same solemn and measured step which had
distinguished him from the first, through the
blue chamber to the purple — through the
purple to the green — through the green to
the orange — through this again to the white
— and even thence to the violet, ere a decided
movement had been made to arrest him. It
was then, however, that the Prince Prospero,
maddening with rage and the shame of his
own momentary cowardice, rushed hurriedly
through the six chambers, while none followed him on account of a deadly terror that
had seized upon all. He bore aloft a drawn
dagger, and had approached, in rapid impetu-

osity, to within three or four feet of the retreating figure, when the latter, having
attained the extremity of the velvet apartment, turned suddenly and confronted his
pursuer. There was a sharp cry — and the
dagger dropped gleaming upon the sable
carpet, upon which, instantly afterward, fell
prostrate in death the Prince Prospero. Then,
summoning the wild courage of despair, a
throng of the revelers at once threw themselves into the black apartment, and, seizing
the mummer, whose tall figure stood erect
and motionless within the shadow of the
ebony clock, gasped in unutterable horror at
finding the grave cerement and corpselike
mask, which they handled with so violent a
rudeness, untenanted by any tangible form.

And now was acknowledged the presence
of the Red Death. He had come like a thief in
the night. And one by one dropped the
revelers in the blood-bedewed halls of their
revel, and died each in the despairing posture
of his fall. And the life of the ebony clock
went out with that of the last of the gay. And
the flames of the tripods expired. And Darkness and Decay and the Red Death held
illimitable dominion over all.

The Imp of
the Perverse

Almost a tale of ratiocination "The Imp of the
Perverse" appeared in *Graham's Magazine* for
July, 1845. As the story begins, an anonymous
narrator (not Poe himself) is in prison, awaiting
execution. He is explaining how he got there. It
seems that he has underestimated the power of
something called "perverseness," which Poe de-
fines as the urge to "act, for the reason that we
should not." Perverseness, says the narrator,
makes people do crazy things, and we must agree
that our minds do double-cross us by "thinking"
of dangerous possibilities, by almost pushing us
into stupid social actions. We tremble as we look
down from a great height, but our perverseness
tempts us to jump. We know we have something
important to do, but perverseness keeps us stal-
ling until it is too late. Perverseness may even
lead a criminal to publish his deeds to the wide
world — and thus sign his own death warrant!

A note on phrenology, the pseudoscience which
claims to discover a man's strong and weak qualities by studying the shape of his head: Poe,
through his narrator, treats phrenology as a re-
spectable science (we would find it hard to agree);
but he complains that phrenologists omit "perverseness" from their charts, and this single
oversight makes their "readings" unreliable.

In the consideration of the faculties and impulses — of the *prima mobilia* of the human soul — the phrenologists have failed to make room for a propensity which, although obviously existing as a radical, primitive, irreducible sentiment, has been equally overlooked by all the moralists who have preceded them. In the pure arrogance of the reason, we have all overlooked it. We have suffered its existence to escape our senses, solely through want of belief — of faith — whether it be faith in Revelation, or faith in the Kabbala. The idea of it has never occured to us, simply because of its supererogation. We saw no *need* of the impulse — for the prosperity. We could not perceive its necessity. We could not understand, that is to say,

we could not have understood, had the notion
of this *primum mobile* ever obtruded itself;
we could not have understood in what manner
it might be made to further the objects of
humanity, either temporal or eternal. It cannot be denied that phrenology and, in great
measure, all metaphysicianism have been concocted *a priori*. The intellectual or logical
man, rather than the understanding or ob-
servant man, set himself to imagine designs
— to dictate purposes to God. Having thus
fathomed, to his satisfaction, the intentions
of Jehovah, out of these intentions he built
his innumerable systems of mind. In the
matter of phrenology, for example, we first
determined, naturally enough, that it was the
design of the Deity that man should eat. We
then assigned to man an organ of alimentive-
ness, and this organ is the scourge with which
the Deity compels man, will-I nill-I, into eat-
ing. Secondly, having settled it to be God's
will that man should continue his species, we
discovered an organ of amativeness, forthwith. And so with combativeness, with ideality, with causality, with constructiveness —
so, in short, with every organ, whether repre-
senting a propensity, a moral sentiment, or a

faculty of the pure intellect. And in these arrangements of the *principia* of human action, the Spurzheimites, whether right or wrong, in part or upon the whole, have but followed, in principle, the footsteps of their predecessors; deducing and establishing everything from the preconceived destiny of man, and upon the ground of the objects of his Creator.

It would have been wiser, it would have been safer, to classify (if classify we must) upon the basis of what man usually of occasionally did, and was always occasionally doing, rather than upon the basis of what we took it for granted the Deity intended him to do. If we cannot comprehend God in his visible works, how then in his inconceivable thoughts, that call the works into being? If we cannot understand him in his objective creatures, how then in his substantive moods and phases of creation?

Induction, *a posteriori*, would have brought phrenology to admit, as an innate, and primitive principle of human action, a paradoxical something, which we may call *perverseness*, for want of a more characteristic term. In the sense I intend, it is, in fact, a *mobile* without

motive, a motive not *motiviert*. Through
its promptings we act without comprehen-
sible object; or, if this shall be understood as
a contradiction in terms, we may so far
modify the proposition as to say that through
its promptings we act, for the reason that we
should *not*. In theory, no reason can be more
unreasonable; but, in fact, there is none more
strong. With certain minds, under certain
conditions, it becomes absolutely irresistible.
I am not more certain that I breathe than
that the assurance of the wrong or error of
any action is often the one unconquerable
force which impels us, and alone impels us,
to its prosecution. Nor will this overwhelm-
ing tendency to do wrong for the wrong's
sake admit of analysis, or resolution into
ulterior elements. It is a radical, a primitive
impulse — elementary. It will be said, I am
aware, that when we persist in acts because
we feel we should *not* persist in them, our
conduct is but a modification of that which
ordinarily springs from the *combativeness* of
phrenology. But a glance will show the fallacy
of this idea. The phrenological combativeness
has for its essence the necessity of self-
defense. It is our safeguard against injury.

Its principle regards our well-being; and
thus the desire to be well excited simultaneously with its development. It follows
that the desire to be well must be excited
simultaneously with any principle which
shall be merely a modification of combativeness; but in the case of that something which
I term *perverseness*, the desire to be well is
not only aroused, but a strongly antagonisti-
cal sentiment exists

An appeal to one's own heart is, after all,
the best reply to the sophistry just noticed.
No one who trustingly consults and
thoroughly questions his own soul will be
disposed to deny the entire radicalness of the
propensity in question. It is not more incomprehensible than distinctive. There lives no
man who at some period has not been tormented, for example, by an earnest desire to
tantalize a listener by circumlocution. The
speaker is aware that he displeases; he has
every intention to please; he is usually curt,
precise, and clear; the most laconic and
luminous language is struggling for utterance upon his tongue; it is only with difficulty
that he restrains himself from giving it flow;
he dreads and deprecates the anger of him

whom he addresses; yet, the thought strikes him, that by certain involutions and parentheses this anger may be engendered. That single thought is enough. The impulse increases to a wish, the wish to a desire, the desire to an uncontrollable longing, and the longing (to the deep regret and mortification of the speaker, and in defiance of all consequences) is indulged.

We have a task before us which must be speedily performed. We know that it will be ruinous to make delay. The most important crisis of our life calls, trumpet-tongued, for immediate energy and action. We glow, we are consumed with eagerness to commence the work, with the anticipation of whose glorious result our whole souls are on fire. It must, it shall be undertaken today, and yet we put it off until tomorrow; and why? There is no answer, except that we feel *perverse,* using the word with no comprehension of the principle. Tomorrow arrives, and with it a more impatient anxiety to do our duty; but with this very increase of anxiety arrives, also, a nameless, a positively fearful, because unfathomable, craving for delay. This craving gathers strength as the moments fly. The

last hour for action is at hand. We tremble
with the violence of the conflict within us, of
the definite with the indefinite, of the substance with the shadow. But, if the contest
has proceeded thus far, it is the shadow
which prevails — we struggle in vain. The
clock strikes, and is the knell of our welfare.
At the same time, it is the chanticleer note to
the ghost that has so long overawed us. It
flies — it disappears — we are free. The old
energy returns. We will labor *now*. Alas, it is
too late!

We stand upon the brink of a precipice. We
peer into the abyss — we grow sick and
dizzy. Our first impulse is to shrink from the
danger. Unaccountably we remain. By slow
degrees our sickness and dizziness and horror
become merged in a cloud of unnamable feeling. By gradations, still more imperceptible,
this cloud assumes shape, as did the vapor
from the bottle out of which arose the genius
in the *Arabian Nights*. But out of this *our*
cloud upon the precipice's edge, there grows
into palpability, a shape, far more terrible
than any genius or any demon of a tale, and
yet it is but a thought, although a fearful one,
and one which chills the very marrow of our

bones with the fierceness of the delight of its horror. It is merely the idea of what would be our sensations during the sweeping precipitancy of a fall from such a height. And this fall, this rushing annihilation, for the very reason that it involves that one most ghastly and loathsome of all the most ghastly and loathsome images of death and suffering which have ever presented themselves to our imagination — for this very cause do we now the most vividly desire it. And because our reason violently deters us from the brink, *therefore* do we the most impetuously approach it. There is no passion in nature so demoniacally impatient as that of him who, shuddering upon the edge of a precipice, thus mediates a plunge. To indulge, for a moment, in any attempt at *thought*, is to be inevitably lost; for reflection but urges us to forbear, and *therefore* it is, I say, that we *cannot*. If there be no friendly arm to check us, or if we fail in a sudden effort to prostrate ourselves backward from the abyss, we plunge, and are destroyed.

Examine these and similar actions as we will, we shall find them resulting solely from the spirit of the *Perverse*. We perpetrate them merely because we feel that we should *not*. Beyond or behind this there is no intelligible principle; and we might, indeed, deem this perverseness a direct instigation of the archfiend, were it not occasionally known to operate in furtherance of good.

I have said thus much, that in some measure I may answer your question — that I may explain to you why I am here — that I may assign to you something that shall have at least the faint aspect of a cause for my wearing these fetters, and for my tenanting this cell of the condemned. Had I not been thus prolix, you might either have misunderstood me altogether, or, with the rabble, have fancied me mad. As it is, you will easily perceive that I am one of the many uncounted victims of the Imp of the Perverse.

It is impossible that any deed could have been wrought with a more thorough deliberation. For weeks, for months, I pondered upon the means of the murder. I rejected a thousand schemes, because their accomplishment involved a *chance* of detection. At length, in reading some French memoirs, I found an account of a nearly fatal illness that occurred to Madame Pilau, through the agency of a candle accidentally poisoned. The idea struck my fancy at once. I knew my victim's habit of reading in bed. I knew, too, that his apartment was narrow and ill-ventilated. But I need not vex you with impertinent details. I need not describe the easy artifices by which I substituted, in his bedroom candle stand, a wax light of my own making for the one which I there found. The next morning he was discovered dead in his bed, and the coroner's verdict was: "Death by the visitation of God."

Having inherited his estate, all went well with me for years. The idea of detection never once entered my brain. Of the remains of the fatal taper I had myself carefully disposed. I had left no shadow of a clue by which it would be possible to convict, or even to suspect, me of the crime. It is inconceivable how rich a sentiment of satisfaction arose in my bosom as I reflected upon my absolute security. For a very long period of time I was accustomed to revel in this sentiment. It afforded me more real delight than all the mere worldly advantages accruing from my sin. But there arrived at length an epoch, from which the pleasurable feeling grew, by

scarcely perceptible gradations, into a haunt-
ing and harassing thought. It harassed because it haunted. I could scarcely get rid of it
for an instant. It is quite a common thing to
be thus annoyed with the ringing in our ears,
or rather in our memories, of the burden of
some ordinary song, or some unimpressive
snatches from an opera. Nor will we be the
less tormented if the song in itself be good, or
the opera air meritorious. In this manner, at
last, I would perpetually catch myself ponder-
ing upon my security, and repeating, in a low
undertone, the phrase, "I am safe."

One day, while sauntering along the
streets, I arrested myself in the act of murmuring, half aloud, these customary syllables.
In a fit of petulance, I remodelled them thus:
"I am safe — I am safe — yes — if I be not
fool enough to make open confession!"

No sooner had I spoken these words than
I felt an icy chill creep to my heart. I had had
some experience in these fits of perversity
(whose nature I have been at some trouble to
explain), and I remembered well that in no
instance had I successfully resisted their
attacks. And now my own casual self-
suggestion, that I might possibly be fool

enough to confess the murder of which I had been guilty, confronted me, as if the very ghost of him whom I had murdered — and beckoned me on to death.

At first, I made an effort to shake off this nightmare of the soul. I walked vigorously — faster — still faster — at length I ran. I felt a maddening desire to shriek aloud. Every succeeding wave of thought overwhelmed me with new terror, for, alas! I well, too well, understood that to *think*, in my situation, was to be lost. I still quickened my pace. I bounded like a madman through the crowded thoroughfares. At length, the populace took the alarm and pursued me. I felt *then* the consummation of my fate. Could I have torn out my tongue, I would have done it; but a rough voice resounded in my ears — a rougher grasp seized me by the shoulder. I turned — I gasped for breath. For a moment I experienced all the pangs of suffocation; I became blind, and deaf, and giddy; and then some invisible fiend, I thought, struck me with his broad palm upon the back. The long-imprisoned secret burst forth from my soul.

They say that I spoke with a distinct enunciation, but with marked emphasis and passionate hurry, as if in dread of interruption before concluding the brief but pregnant sentences that consigned me to the hangman and to hell.

Having related all that was necessary for the fullest judicial conviction, I fell prostrate in a swoon.

But why shall I say more? Today I wear these chains, and am *here!* Tomorrow I shall be fetterless! — *but where?*